THE WORK RETREAT

A GRIPPING AND UNPUTDOWNABLE PSYCHOLOGICAL THRILLER

SL HARKER

1

Is there anything more destructive than obsession—the kind that destroys your sense of right and wrong, that seeps into every thought, making it impossible to think straight? I'm at our annual work retreat with my colleagues sitting around me, and all I can see is him. My married boss. The man I can't stop crushing over. It's sick. It's stupid. I'm thirty, and I should know better. But I guess that's what happens when you've been a walking wound for so long.

Nathan's eyes stumble onto mine. It's brief, a millisecond at best, but electric heat bolts up my spine like a firecracker. I'm the first to break eye contact, shuffling my gaze to my lap as warmth spreads from my neck to my face. I'm sure I'm the color of a ripe tomato, and a whole room of my coworkers are here to witness my shame.

He clears his throat and speaks, the vibrato of his voice dripping like sap through the small banquet room. "So, folks, we are going to try this team-building exercise to see where we stand with the marketing process for several products.

We're projecting major sales this month, but it all depends on how we get our ads out there to the key demographics."

I keep my chin down, my eyes focused on the white-triangle print of my navy blue dress. Sweat dampens the fabric, making it stick to my skin. *What happened to the air conditioning?* I purposefully look at my colleagues instead of my boss, Vivian, who is all dark hair and good skin. Seriously, in her mid-forties, she's more gorgeous than ever. She nods along as Nathan speaks.

Be like Vivian. Do your job.

The thing is, I'm trying to earn my stripes here at Cutler-Stewart, a mid-size advertising company. At thirty, I'm the junior member of the marketing team, and a lot of the time, I feel as if some of the more seasoned employees are sizing me up, figuring out whether I'll sink or swim.

Chet scoffs at something Nathan says, and it pulls me back to reality. Whether the sound is intentional or not, it's hard to tell. I sense Nathan's spine straightening and his cobalt-blue eyes darkening into storm clouds. A ripple of tension slips across his jawline.

"Is there some insight you'd like to add to the group?" Nathan asks Chet.

Janine's mouth makes an *O*. So much tension has been building between Chet and Nathan, and now, in this cheap room in a cheap hotel two hours outside Chicago, it ripples to the surface.

But Chet is never ruffled or embarrassed. He shrugs. "No. Carry on." Then he grins and adds, "Boss."

Nathan is our team leader. He organized the retreat. Considering the tension within the team, he thought it would be a good idea for us to get out of the office. But seriously, did he have to bring us to this bumfuck town in the middle of nowhere? I don't think I've seen a single stop light here.

"Well, thank you, Chet. I will."

We all cringe now. I pick up a pen and tap it lightly against the polished mahogany table. Even though I am relatively new to the game, I've heard whispers that Chet is prepared to steal Nathan's job out from under him. The atmosphere thickens, and the two men stare at each other as if wanting to put the other in checkmate.

My stupid lizard brain turns this red flag into a green one. I can't help but think Nathan is hot when he's mad about something. Anger suits him. He's forty-five, but he could pass for thirty-five. He already looks like an Abercrombie & Fitch model, and the temper gives him an edge. He's clean-shaven and tall, with impeccable jet-black hair slicked into a neat side part.

Chet's smile is snide as he shakes his head and wipes his mouth with a handkerchief that he plucked from the breast pocket of his expensive black suit. He has a mop of wavy chestnut hair.

Nathan cuts him a dubious glance but continues. He reaches for his own water glass, his hands once again brushing mine, making my skin tingle. I examine the documents in front of me, determined to focus on the tasks at hand, but it's going to be a major challenge to keep it together.

My mom died several weeks ago. Since then, I've been aware of this gaping hole that never existed before. The world is off-kilter, and the only way I can right it again is to fill the hollowness inside.

Before Mom died, I knew I liked Nathan, but I wasn't obsessed like I am now. I crave him, hoping that being with someone I really like will fill the abyss. I want to stop thinking about death. I need to feel alive again and forget about the disease that took her away.

After the meeting, Nathan takes us all to the hotel bar to chill. It's obvious he feels guilty about snapping at Chet. Personally, I think Chet's sucky attitude is his own problem. The neon sign on the adjacent wall glows brightly. Blue and yellow light dances across the surface of the bar. I order a martini and consider downing it.

Vivian perches like a parrot on her stool, her shoulders stiff. I try to think of how to carry on a conversation with her without it involving tons of awkward silences. We've never been close.

"What did you make of the meeting?" I ask.

She picks at a beer label with a thumbnail. "Whatever Nathan wants, I guess."

Pretty noncommittal. Part of me wonders if I should pick a side, figuring out who is for Chet and who is for Nathan.

"Do you think Chet wants Nathan's job? It got really tense in there."

Vivian lets out a snort. "Don't worry. They'll measure each other's dicks soon enough and put the whole business to bed."

I can't help it—I burst into a fit of giggles. Vivian isn't usually so sassy. Our laughter brings Nathan over. He pulls out a barstool to my left, its metal legs skidding across the wood-planked floor. In the background, a country song plays from an illuminated jukebox.

"Having fun?" he asks.

I bite my lower lip, trying not to think about Nathan and Chet with rulers. I nod, and Vivian fails to smother a laugh.

"I'm going to call it a night." She casts a glance at Chet, who is sitting with Janine, eyeballing us. "Three beers are enough for me."

When she's out the door, Nathan raises an eyebrow. "She drank three beers in a half hour?"

"Yup," I say, smiling. "Vivian does not play."

He laughs and shakes his head. To our left, a group of bearded flannel-clad men play pool.

Nathan plants his elbows on the bar. "So, *are* you having fun? Or do I suck at this cool-boss-at-a-work-retreat thing?"

"I'm having fun. You don't suck." I tuck a lock of hair behind my ear. "But why the hell did you choose this place?"

He laughs. "I got a good deal. The company is trying to save money."

I nod. "I figured."

Nathan glances in Chet's direction. "It's not common knowledge, so don't spread it around."

"I won't."

"Though, I guess it's obvious." Nathan nudges his chin toward the bartender. "I'll take a whiskey sour. Another round of whatever she's having."

"Martini."

Nathan's eyes glint. He studies me as if seeing me for the first time. "Nice choice. You're pretty bold, aren't you, Lucy Croft?"

He's flirting with me. Nathan has never flirted with me before. My face warms with embarrassment.

"I guess." *Bold* has never been a word applied to me. *Bookish*, yes. *Shy*, yes. *Stupid*... okay, that's my word.

"You had some great ideas earlier," Nathan says, bringing the rim of his whiskey glass to his lips.

"Thank you. I enjoy the job."

"You're a natural," Nathan says.

"At advertising?" I grin. "Lucky me. Of all the things to be good at."

Nathan catches my eye, and he lets out a chuckle. I like this side of him. There is something easygoing about Nathan when he's not in work mode.

He shifts his weight, and his musky scent invades my personal space. My heart gallops. His eyes reach mine and linger. When he gives me that charming smile, it's like staring into the surface of the sun.

"We're going back to our rooms." Chet's voice breaks the tension. I almost let out a sigh of relief.

"Sorry again, Chet," Nathan says. "I didn't mean to snap. See you both at breakfast."

Chet and Janine wave goodbye and head out of the bar. I like Janine, but I worry about her hanging around Chet. He's not a gentleman.

"Don't apologize to that douche canoe," I blurt.

Nathan stares at me.

Oh, shit. I called my colleague a douche canoe in front of my very temperamental boss. Shit. Shit. Shit.

He lets out the biggest belly laugh I've ever heard. It spreads to me, and I find myself tearing up. It's a good minute or so before we both calm down.

"Chet's not so bad," Nathan says once the laughter fit fades out. "But I wish he'd stop with all the macho crap. You know?"

I sip my martini. The air settles around us. From nowhere, Nathan reaches across and places his hand over mine.

"I don't know if I've said this, but I was so sorry to hear about your mom. Obviously, I didn't know her, but I lost my mom when I was young. It's a loss I never recovered from."

His words hit me like a sledgehammer. My eyes fill, and I sniff, trying desperately to stop the tears from falling. One escapes, and Nathan leans over, stroking it away with his pinkie.

I exhale a slow breath and whisper, "Thank you."

As we lock eyes, I know this isn't going to end well. How could it? He's my boss. He has a wife. There's nothing more destructive than out-of-control obsession, and here's the thing—I'm not in control anymore.

2

The martini isn't doing me any favors. I mean, technically, it *is* helping soothe the butterflies pattering around inside my stomach every time Nathan's eyes burn into mine. But it's also lowering my inhibitions, making me feel like my insides are made of gooey caramel.

As we remain in the hotel bar, chatting, I try not to appear desperate. Yet my eyes drift to his large, strong hands, noting the way he cradles the glass of whiskey. I pull my hair to one side, letting the nape of my neck cool.

After my third martini, I realize I'm openly flirting. He's good company. He maintains eye contact as we talk. He's engaging, but he doesn't interrupt.

"Has anyone ever told you that you have the most beautiful hair?"

Heat floods my cheeks. I watch him watching me, his hand half lifted as though to touch my hair.

"No," I say. And it's true. While my hair is a soft shade of red now, back at school, it blazed like fire, and all the school kids called me "ginger."

He clears his throat. "Damn. The whiskey is good here. I've had too many, I think. Sorry, Luce. I should go to my room before..."

Before what? I think. But I don't say it out loud.

My martini glass is empty, and my legs are wobbly. It's time for me to go, too. I wait a moment or two, and then follow him out of the bar.

When I see him waiting for the elevator, I almost head toward the stairs. But then I don't. I stand next to him. He doesn't say a word. The bell chimes, the doors part, and we step into the small space together.

Nathan stands at one side of the elevator, and I stand at the other. We don't look at each other. We can't. I wonder if his heart is beating as fast as mine.

"Are you on the fifth floor?" His voice croaks, and he swipes his forehead with the back of his hand. It comes away glistening.

"Yes," I whisper.

The bell chimes. We stumble out of the elevator. We're side-by-side. His hand grazes mine.

Fuck. Fuck. Fuck.

There's a slight ridge in the carpet, and I lose my balance, stumbling into him. The body contact is all we need. He spins me around until my palms are flat against his chest. He gazes down at me as if I'm a snack—or a full-out meal.

It's a mistake, my mind says. *Don't do it.*

And then his hands are in my hair. My arms are around his neck. I tilt my head and lift my chin. My eyelids flutter, and before I can inhale, my lips collide with his. Nathan tastes like honey and salt. His breath is cool on my cheek. His fingers tunnel through my hair. He groans, pinning me against the wall.

Then nothing. He pulls away first. I stand there, embarrassed, my hair mussed and dress rumpled. He takes me in like he's in a daze, staring at me with wild eyes.

"What are we doing?" he says as though to himself.

"I'm sorry," I whisper. "You're right. We should... you're my boss and..." The alcohol surges through my veins, yet I feel sharp as a tack, as if everything is in focus.

I start to walk away, but Nathan cuffs his hand over my wrist and pulls me back. "Wait... Lucy, I... oh, fuck it."

Our bodies clash together, a tangle of hands and mouths. Somehow, we make our way down the hall. Nathan grabs a hotel keycard from his pocket, and we cross the threshold into his room. He leaves the light off, with nothing but moonlight to guide us.

I concentrate on touch—the ruggedness of his large hands palming my breasts under my dress. The way his fingers slip sensually under my panties with an urgency that leaves me trembling. His touch is like icy heat between my legs, making me lightheaded.

"Fuck, you're hot," he murmurs.

His breath is feverish as he exhales against my cheek. His hands journey to my waist, shoving my dress up around my hips. He pins me to the wall again, pressing his weight against me. I let out a sigh of pleasure as his hands circle my wrists. His mouth is hungry on mine. My teeth sink into his bottom lip. He groans, almost growling.

He drops my wrists to pull the dress over my head. A second later, one hand reaches behind me to unclasp my bra. Then my legs are around his waist as he lifts me with ease. Hands weave through my hair. His jacket comes off, followed by his tie, guided by my fingers. I fumble through the buttons, finally feeling his warm flesh, my nails raking down his shoulder blades. And like that, half-undressed, he carries me to the bed.

From here, we're only two silhouettes intertwined under the milky moonlight streaming in from the cracks in the curtains. *We could be anyone.*

And this is what I choose to think about as he buries his head between my legs and his lips part my sensitive flesh. His tongue finds my throbbing clit, and he gives the swollen area gentle kisses that make me moan, arch my back, and press my thighs around his head.

As I reach the point of no return, he slows down the insistence of the kisses—most definitely to edge me on purpose. His tongue glides in glorious mind-melting circles, parting my crevices and folds. I dig my heels into his torso, and my climax violently shudders from me, a breathy moan escaping my lips.

Now that my eyes have adjusted to the light, I see that Nathan is grinning, his eyes gleaming under the silver moon. I wonder whether this is the way he looks at his wife when he makes love to her or if he has saved this enthusiasm only for me. The thought makes my stomach flip, and I push it away. His kisses don't lose their luster as he snakes his way back up to my face, his lips leaving a trail from my navel to my bare breasts.

He undresses quickly. His movements are desperate as he reaches for a condom then tosses his wallet aside, along with his pants. He sheaths the condom on and whispers in my ear that we need to be careful. I nod as his fingers spread across my hips and he turns me around so that I'm on all fours, facing the headboard.

I feel him, swollen and pulsing on my inner thighs. I want him so badly, I could scream. I brace my hands on the headboard for support as he enters me and grinds our hips together, slowly at first, and then blissfully, he cranks it up a notch.

I can't see his face. I want to see him, to hold his gaze. But when I turn to face him, he grabs hold of my hair and pulls my head back. I let out a gasp of surprise. He holds me so tight, I can barely move. And then he thrusts, each time shoving me deeper and deeper into the bed. This is what I wanted. I wanted him inside me. Is it everything I hoped for?

He pushes my face down into the sheet, his weight pressing on top of me. My hands ball the soft cotton, and I'm lost—in him, in myself, and in the world. Panic rushes through me at the realization of what I'm doing. I feel his body stiffen. His cock is rock-hard inside me. He groans, squeezes my ass, and he slams into me, hard, grunting, until he's completely on top of me and it's over.

He collapses beside me. Slowly, I pull myself out from the sheet, tugging it over my naked body. Nathan disappears into the bathroom, no doubt to clean himself up.

What have I done?

I know what I did. I fucked my boss. I fucked my *married* boss.

"You okay?"

I didn't hear him come back into the room, but he climbs into the bed, naked. He lifts a fatigued arm and sweeps the hair away from my eyes and cheeks. The gesture is tender. Sweet.

"I'm okay," I reply. "I was miles away."

"Listen, I want you to know that didn't come out of nowhere. I do like you."

"Thanks, that means a lot," I reply. And I mean it. "But it's okay. If you want... if this is all..." I give up trying to explain myself and place a hand on my forehead.

"I know." He kisses the tip of my nose.

He turns over and pulls me into his body. I twist myself so that we spoon, and for a moment, I can pretend we're more than boss and employee, man and mistress. I can pretend we're together like a real couple. Tomorrow, my mind will be ransacked by guilt. In the light of day, it will be different for me and for Nathan. But for now, in the darkness, I'll let him reach for my hand and hold it. I'll stay naked with him, reveling in how good it feels to get caught up in the fantasy, ignoring the dread sitting low and sour in the pit of my belly.

I glance up at the digital clockface on the bedside table. The time reads 2:08. Mom always told me that nothing good ever happened after two in the morning. I can't help but think she was right.

3

I know it's still early because it's dark. It takes me a moment to acclimatize, especially with the sleeping lump beside me. Nathan. His chest rises and falls, nice and steady. I'm not sure why it tickles me to see he's a stomach sleeper. My head throbs, reminding me of the three—or was it four? —martinis I drank last night. I glance at the sharp red numbers of his bedside clock. It's 5:09.

Careful not to disturb the bed too much, I peel the sheets away from the lower half of my body, cringing when I realize I'm still naked. *How could I have allowed this to happen?*

Fragments of our steamy, sexy encounter ambush my mind out of nowhere. Nathan's hands on my breasts. His mouth hungrily devours mine. His breath tickling my cheek and neck as he groaned in my ear. The musky scent of his intoxicating cologne. The weight of him as he pressed me deep into the bed and how I'd enjoyed surrendering to him.

Yet even then, I felt something alongside the lust, a recognition that beamed brighter at five in the morning than it had last night. We didn't just fuck. It was frenzied, almost unhealthy. I can't strip the images from my mind. They haunt as much as titillate. I find myself reeling, hurrying away from the bed. I need to get out of this room.

I remind myself to go stealthily. I don't want Nathan to wake up and see me leaving. I want to slip out like a ghost in the night, leaving without a trace. As my eyes adjust to the darkness, I scan the room for my dress and locate it in a corner next to Nathan's side of the bed.

I pad around the end of the bed and step up in front of him. Nathan grunts and rubs his face, making a low snorting sound. I freeze in place, afraid he will open his eyes and see me standing there, naked. But he doesn't. He rolls over, coughs, and tugs the sheets up around his body.

I exhale a slow, quiet breath, reach down for my dress, and pluck it from the floor. I sling the garment over my head in the darkness.

After tiptoeing to the door, I check once more behind me and gently turn the handle. I allow myself a quick sigh of relief when I'm out of that room. The lights are harsh and bright in the hallway. It could be a spotlight, like I'm on a stage, unclothed, and the audience is made up of disgruntled wives. "Here she is," says the host, "the woman who sleeps with married men." I picture them booing and throwing rotten fruit. And I would deserve it.

Back in my own hotel room, I get a good look at my reflection. I'm a hot mess. I have what Grannie Croft called racoon eyes from smudged mascara. I've never seen my hair *this* frizzy before, and that's impressive, considering the natural waves I inherited from said grandma. The navy dress I ironed before packing is wrinkled and sweat stained. Worst of all, a dull migraine pulses between my eyes and temples.

"What the hell is wrong with you?" I glare at my mirror

self then twist on the shower nozzle and stare at my reflection until the steam from the hot water cloaks me like a heavy fog. I embrace the mist, wanting to disappear into it, leaving all my shame behind.

⌐

"You aren't touching your fruit," Vivian notes, pointing to the colorful plate that I got from the free breakfast buffet.

"Huh?" I blink at her, my fingers coiled around a warm mug of coffee. I've decided that coffee is my new best friend. I've broken up with martinis. They lead to bad, bad decisions. Also, coffee is the only thing settling my queasy stomach.

"Holy fuck. What the hell happened to you?" She parks her behind on the chair next to mine.

"Do I look that awful?"

"Yes, honey. You do. What happened last night?"

I freeze. While changing before breakfast, I toyed with the idea of leaving so I didn't have to face Nathan again. But then everyone might guess what happened between us. I figured staying to face the music would be my least suspicious action, but I hadn't factored in how obvious my hangover would be.

"Martinis," I say. "I don't know what came over me."

"You and Nathan were getting pretty cozy when I left."

"Ew," I say, recoiling. "Actually"—I lean closer—"I kinda went back to my room with one of those cowboys. You know, the pool guys?"

"Oh, you bad girl." Vivian grins.

"Do *not* tell anyone," I say, wagging a finger.

Vivian places a hand on her chest. "I would never!"

Well, I guess that's one issue dealt with for now. I'm going to have to suck it up and get through the rest of this nightmare as best I can. I've already vowed to myself that I'm going to avoid Nathan at all costs. I don't need to keep going down this road. The stakes are too high. Too many people, myself included, could end up hurt.

"Don't you want it?" she asks, gesturing to the food on my plate.

My eyes shift downward. "Oh. Well, I'm not as hungry as I thought."

"Can I have it, then?"

"Sure." I push the plate in her direction.

"Rough night?" Janine asks, approaching the table, her gaze set on me.

I groan. "Not you, too. Seriously?"

Her long, shiny black hair is perfectly blown out, as usual. Her face is glowing, cheeks rosy, and eye makeup impeccable. Janine slides into the empty chair beside me, and I bristle, hoping she doesn't notice. Her perfume is flowery and pleasant but cloying when combined with my hangover. Janine is the office administrator. She's even younger than I am, early twenties, and she's full of energy—too much energy for me to handle when I'm hungover and questioning my life choices.

"Yeah, me too, sort of," she says.

Vivian chimes in. "Lucy took a cowboy back to her hotel room."

I lift my hands in the air. "Are you for real?"

"What? It's just us girls. I thought you meant don't tell Nathan."

"No, Vivian, I meant do not tell *anyone*."

But the truth is, Vivian did me a favor. Janine loves drama and would have interrogated me anyway. Now at least, she has an answer to her inevitable questions.

Janine's blue eyes widen, and her lipstick-painted mouth forms a perfect oval when she squeals. She bumps her shoulder into mine. "One of the pool guys, huh? The cute one with the sandy hair?"

I slink back in my chair and swallow hard, staring at my lap. "Yup."

My heart hammers, worried Janine will see through my bold-faced lie, but she swirls her coffee stick around in her cup and gives me a superficial pout, her eyes lighting up. "So, did he text?"

"What?" I ask, distracted by a wave of nausea.

"You got his number, right?"

"Actually, no. It was a one-time thing."

She rubs my back, purring, clearly delighted to learn I failed to make the guy interested enough to get my number. "Oh, that's okay, sweetie. Maybe next time," she says in a satisfied tone.

If she only knew that I'd slept with our boss. No. She can *never* know.

I shrug. "Oh well. It's fine."

Janine bobs her head up and down as if she's trying to relate to me, but I see right through it. She is competitive as all hell with other women. Now she gets to see herself as superior for *always* getting a guy to call the next day. It's written all over her face. Well, whatever distracts her from finding out I slept with Nathan.

I push myself away from the table, balancing the coffee in one hand and sliding my purse over my shoulder with the other. "We should get to the first team-building exercise."

"Sure, I guess I'd better hurry up." Janine grins at me and winks. "Maybe I can be your wing woman at the bar tonight, and we can both score. I need to get laid. *Bad.*"

I didn't need to know that, but I give her a commiserative smile. Through clenched teeth, I say, "Yeah, maybe," knowing I have no intention of setting foot outside my hotel room after working hours.

Last night was too close for comfort. They all saw me chatting and drinking with Nathan at the bar. If they hadn't bought my story about the guy playing pool, they would have guessed what really happened for sure. And then what? Would I lose my job—or worse, would it break up Nathan's marriage? There's no way Chet wouldn't jump on the opportunity to use it to his advantage.

It's time for me to backpedal on my mistakes. For the duration of this trip, it's going to be nothing but cheesy Lifetime movies on the TV while I scarf Chinese takeout straight from the carton on my hotel bed.

4

At every team-building exercise, I make sure to sit as far away from Nathan as possible. I never dare to make eye contact with him, and I don't offer insight on any ideas unless I'm in a group setting where Nathan isn't involved. Miraculously, I get through every icebreaker and trust exercise. Every brainstorming session. Every problem-solving task.

And he clearly has the same idea. I'm almost offended by how far away from me he stays. Until, of course, I think about his wife and kids.

By the end of it all, I'm like a tightly stretched rubber band ready to snap. All I want is to go home and forget this ever happened. Only that's impossible because I'm still plagued with the vivid memories of what Nathan did to me on that sweaty, sexy night in his hotel room.

Friday can't come fast enough. I don't know how many more times I can lie to Janine and tell her I have a migraine or stomach ache, whatever it takes to get me off the hook from going to the bar with her. That morning, I wake, thinking about how nice it will be to not have to see Nathan around every corner and be constantly reminded of our frenzied fucking, the weight of his body on mine, the feel of his hands holding my wrists or yanking my hair.

Then I remember I don't have my car. Nathan drove me here. *Fuck.* He's my ride back to civilization. Three hours in a car, sitting right next to the man I want to ride until I can't walk. *Shit.* But Janine rode with us on the way here. I'd almost forgotten. She sat in the back, napping the entire journey as I daydreamed about my sexy boss.

I zip shut the suitcase and let out a sigh of relief. Janine may be a lot to handle, but at least she'll be the buffer between me and Nathan that I desperately need. My stomach roils as I wheel the suitcase out of the hotel room. This, without a doubt, has been the worst work trip I've ever been on. And I suddenly feel so lonely that I wish I had my mom to call.

"Need a hand?" Chet, not Nathan, is in the hall. It's the first time I've ever been relieved to see him.

"I've got it," I say. "But thanks."

"You've been like a ghost these last few days. Went too hard on the first night, huh?"

"Something like that."

"Well, I for one am glad we're going. There's no pussy within ten miles of this place." He glances at me. "Present company excluded."

I sigh. "Seriously, Chet. You're a walking sexual-harassment case."

He laughs. "Sorry. I am trying to rein that in." For a moment, he sounds sincere. Then he takes the suitcase from my hand and wheels it along the hallway for me. "Hey, has

Nathan mentioned anything to you about whether he's moving on?"

"No, why? Has he said something to you?"

Chet shakes his head. "I guess he seems off. Like his heart isn't in it. The first day, he was all fired up, and then he barely supervised us. We came up with—what, two decent ideas this whole trip? And both of them were mine."

I roll my eyes. "I don't know about that. Maybe he's under a lot of pressure."

"Oh, he is, for sure. The shareholders are not happy right now."

The elevator dings, and we step in. Janine and Vivian are already inside with their suitcases. Vivian nods. Janine barely glances up from her phone. Chet promptly shuts up before spilling any more interesting nuggets of information. I had no idea about the shareholders. I knew we'd lost a big client recently and that there'd been some scrambling to recover the lost income, but I didn't know things were that bad.

Which puts a different spin on my crazy one-night stand with Nathan. He probably wanted to blow off steam. It wasn't about me. He didn't like me or want to be with me. He took something from me that he couldn't get from his wife at the time. I was a fucking stress ball.

"Hey, Luce," Janine says from behind me. I turn to face her. "I don't need a ride anymore. Can you tell Nathan?"

"What? Why?"

"Because," she begins slowly then twirls her long hair around in her finger, a signature habit I've noticed. "I'm going to meet up with a friend who lives nearby. We have a lot of catching up to do, if you know what I mean." She winks.

As much as this makes me cringe, I can't hide my disappointment. "Can't you do that another time?" The words blurt from me before my brain has a chance to react and stop them.

"What's with the tone?" Janine asks. "And why do you even care? The retreat is over, and the weekend is about to start. I'm allowed to do something else besides work, you know."

I backpedal, giving her a casual smile, although it's a struggle to force it. "Oh. Yeah. Totally. No, that's cool."

"Yeah, Lucy, let the girl get laid," Chet adds. "Prude."

My face flushes. "I'm not..." I shake my head, deciding to let them think I'm a prude. "I hope you have a good time with your... friend." I smile at Janine, hoping to repair the fracture.

The elevator doors open, and I see Nathan checking out of the hotel. *Three hours alone in a car with him.* My throat goes dry.

5

"That's the last one." I step aside so Nathan can close the trunk. "By the way, Janine isn't riding with us. She, erm, she's going to meet a friend who lives nearby."

Nathan exhales a deep breath. "Well, I guess it's just me and you, then."

I brave a glance at him. He's wearing an apprehensive grin, but I can tell he's trying to be polite and let me carve the path of the conversation.

"Yeah, I, uh—I guess so." I tuck a strand of hair behind my ear and feel an onset of heat rushing up my neck to my cheeks. I lower my chin and pretend to inspect something on the ground so he won't see my face stained red.

"Lucy..." Nathan's voice is barely above a whisper.

"Hmm?" I look at him again.

Nathan opens his mouth but quickly clamps it shut, as though he wants to tell me something but doesn't know where to begin. He walks around to the driver's side, his face pale. "Are you ready to head back?"

"When you are." I shrug, but my heart has jumped into my throat, and I can't swallow it back down.

His car is immaculate, but it's so hot inside that my legs stick to the tan leather. I peel them off and adjust myself to get comfortable, keeping my body angled away from Nathan. I stare out the window as he reverses out of the spot. *Is the entire journey going to be this awkward?* Yes, I realize, when after a half hour we're still silent.

As Nathan turns onto the on ramp for the interstate, his gaze cuts to me. "You want to listen to music?"

"Sure." *Finally.*

"Anything in particular?"

"Not really." My voice is hollow and distant.

Nathan licks his lips, gripping the steering wheel tighter. "Listen, Lucy, I've been meaning to talk to you about what happened between us..."

I stare out the window. "Okay." I don't look at him, but I hear him sigh and see his shoulders sink in my peripheral vision.

"Don't take this the wrong way, but what we did the other night, well, it just can't happen again."

Even though I expected him to say it, I still find myself turning to study the frame of his face in the sunlight, the way his aviators make him resemble an adventurer, and the slight five-o'clock shadow along his jaw.

"I know. It's okay. I understand." My voice is even, betraying no emotion, giving me hope that I can handle this car ride after all.

Nathan regards me, but I can't see his eyes through the sunglasses. "Are you okay?"

"I'm fine." I cradle my hands in my lap.

"My marriage is hitting a bit of a rough patch right now

and—"

"Nathan." I offer an empathetic smile. "You don't have to explain yourself. We both had a lack of judgment that night."

His features slacken with relief, and he rubs his forehead with the tips of his fingers. "Thank you for being so cool about this. I mean, don't get me wrong—it was *great*, but..."

Sex is always great when it's happening. It's the regret afterward that is hard to live with. That urge to call Mom returns. I ball my hands into fists to stop myself from crying. I don't want Nathan thinking I'm crying over him.

When I don't talk, he continues trying to spout off reasons for rejecting me. "I really want to try to make it work with my wife."

"Really?" I arch a cynical eyebrow. I'm not trying to argue with him, but the way he says it is watered down, as if he's trying to convince himself.

He watches me for a moment then glances back at the road. When he speaks again, his voice is cautious. "Yes. It's just. You know, having twins—it's a lot of work. More than I realized. It's made things difficult between me and Angela."

"I'm sorry to hear that." I stare out the window, but the heat of Nathan's gaze burns through me.

"I never meant for any of this to happen." He sounds apologetic. This whole conversation is so pathetic that I want a hole to open up right here inside this car so I can shrivel inside it and disappear. Forever.

"What we did was inappropriate," I say, not sure how else to respond. "It's best to forget all about it." *Holy crap. I wish Janine was in this car right now.*

Nathan rubs his chin and becomes pensive, staring straight ahead. We come to a bottleneck of traffic. Nathan drums his fingertips against the steering wheel and fidgets in his seat. Something about his repetitive movements rub me the wrong way. Maybe it's the heat or the feeling of being trapped.

"Don't worry. I won't hit on you again." Too late, I realize I'm unable to hide the bitterness in my voice. My stupid brain let me blurt the words without thinking.

Nathan turns to me. "What's that supposed to mean?"

"It means you don't have to act desperate to get away from me."

"I'm not doing that. I'm just frustrated with the traffic." He jabs at a few buttons on the navigation panel, and the robotic voice offers us an alternate route to avoid the traffic jam. Nathan gets off at the next exit and floors the gas pedal.

I grind my knees into the door and dig my nails into the side of my seat. "Take it easy, I want to get home alive."

Nathan eases his foot off the gas, but every corner has me sliding from side to side. "Why are you angry all of a sudden?"

"I'm not angry. But I will be if you wreck this car and kill me."

"I'm in control, Lucy," he snaps.

I wonder if that's true. From the way we had sex the other night, it's clear that Nathan likes taking control. But right now, he's rattled, and I don't know him well enough to know how he reacts when he feels that way. I'm relieved to see him slow down. I rest my forehead against the window and settle in for the rest of the journey.

We ride like that in silence for a few miles, then the GPS voice declares, "Signal lost."

Nathan swears and presses a button. The navigation screen goes blank. Outside the window, I see nothing but fields and dirt tracks. In the middle of our argument, I never noticed that we'd ended up in the middle of nowhere.

6

Nathan taps the screen two more times before letting out a slow exhalation.

"What's wrong?" My scalp prickles as though reacting to some predatory instinct I can't see.

He doesn't answer, instead pulling over and cutting the engine.

I press my fingers to the window, staring out at fields of corn. "Are we lost?"

His shoulders rise and fall rapidly, and he's taking quick, shallow breaths. He removes his sunglasses, his eyes darting to the windows, wide and frantic. "How the hell should I know?"

I slink into my seat. "Okay, calm down."

Nathan jabs his finger into the screen, growling. "Damn it!"

"Let's head back to the interstate. It can't be far."

"If we can find it," he says. "You distracted me so much, I can't remember which way we came, and there aren't any fucking signs around here."

"Oh, sure, blame me. Pathetic."

"Not helping, Lucy."

"Well, neither are you!" I shout.

"The GPS went out!" Nathan bellows. Beads of sweat form at his temples. "What are the changes?" He calms for a moment, craning his neck to see the sky outside the window. "Maybe it's going to storm or something. Or there's some sort of issue with a satellite." He scoffs. "This *never* happens. But it happened with you."

"Right. I broke the GPS, did I? What, do you think I'm some sort of bunny boiler trying to keep you alone with me? Fuck no. I want out of this car, and I want to be away from you." I reach for the door handle, but he grabs my hand.

"You know what, Lucy?"

A bolt of lightning shoots up my spine. He glares at me as if he wants to destroy me and fuck me all at once.

"What?" I bark, holding his gaze.

"You just—you—" He groans and tunnels his fingers through his hair.

He has a wide, vulnerable expression, like a hopeless little boy. It makes me ache to console him. A puff of air escapes his parted lips.

His eyes soften on me. "I'm sorry. I'm not myself. I'm not in the right headspace. I'm frustrated and taking it out on you."

I'm startled by both his vulnerability and his apology. Powerful men don't tend to apologize, and it catches me off guard. Every muscle in my body tightens, like I'm scared to move. We've finally stopped arguing, and I don't want to ruin the moment.

He reaches out and caresses my cheek with two fingers. Then a thumb. And then both hands are in my hair. I'm not sure who kisses the other first or whether it's simultaneous, but we kiss, and it's feverish and urgent.

"I'm sorry, Lucy," he murmurs between satisfied groans. "I'm so sorry."

All resolve to do better, to be better, is gone. I plunge into the darkest cavity of desire, surrendering to him. It feels so good. If I'm honest with myself, this is what I want, this feeling—the kind that blocks out pain and switches off every thought.

His fingers fumble with my lace bra, while his other hand shakily unbuttons my shorts. I hear his zipper go down. He pulls his cock out, the tip glistening, ready for me. I cuff my fist around his rock-hard shaft and stroke it.

His eyes roll in pleasure. My ego soars, my fingers coiled around his girth and tightening with each seductive stroke.

"You drive me crazy," he whispers into my neck.

I rake my nails across his scalp and rub my fingertips across his broad muscular shoulders. His biceps flex as his hands journey south, skidding across my thighs, pushing my shorts and panties down around my ankles. I toss them off with a shake of my feet.

The temptation is in full swing. There's no turning back now. The heat, the electricity, the tension between us crackles and snaps.

Nathan's fingers slip between my sensitive folds, rubbing each crease and crevice, finding my clit, caressing it. I'm breathless, dizzy with desire. I help him wiggle his pants down around his thighs and slide across my seat to sit on his lap. With my thighs straddling him, my palms pressed to his chest under his shirt, and my mouth locked to his, Nathan fondles me, his finger inside me up to the knuckle.

"You're so wet." His eyes glaze over. "Baby, I want to fuck you so bad."

I'm so turned on I can't see straight.

"You're a naughty girl, and I love it," Nathan says, his lips fluttering across my collar bone.

I stiffen as warmth spreads through my body, starting in my stomach then surging through my veins. Stars shoot around in front of my vision, and I feel a gush, my pelvic muscles contracting as I'm invaded by a mind-altering orgasm.

I grind my hips on Nathan's hand as he thrusts one finger inside me while another strokes my engorged flesh. I'm throbbing and soaked for him. I gasp for air, weak, my legs like jelly.

Nathan shows me no mercy. He reaches for a condom from his wallet. I know what he said last time—he wants to be careful. It seems like he doesn't even want the kids he already has. I don't care. It's none of my business. I just want him to fuck me until I can't breathe. Nothing else matters. Not the wife, not the kids, not my morals. The lust infected my brain, spreading like a disease.

Nathan grabs his cock, pulsing against my bare thigh. He keeps eye contact as he enters me. I bend my head and press my forehead to his as the windows steam. We rock back and forth together, silently, the only sound in the car is our quick breathing.

I grab the headrest behind him for support as I bounce. Beneath me, Nathan whimpers. I kiss him and caress his hair with tender hands, comforting movements. He stiffens, and a moment later, with a groan of pleasure, it's over. I stop moving, hugging him close.

We sit there together, our eyes locked. I feel him softening inside me and our sweating foreheads touching each other. Here comes the instant regret—the shame invading my body. No, not shame, something worse. The truth is, I can't control myself when I'm with him, and it seems as though he can't control himself, either. What's wrong with us? Why are we like this? It isn't love. I don't know him deeply enough to love him. Sure, we've worked together for a while, but during that time, all I did was crush on him from afar. We never had a connection.

This realization spreads a hot fear through me that cracks through my chest like molten lava. *I'm not myself. Who am I?*

I don't have time to figure it out because I hear a car in the distance.

7

"Do you hear that?" The hairs on the nape of my neck stand on end.

Nathan tilts his head, his eyes narrowed. I'm still sitting on his lap, with his huge hands planted on either side of my hips. With the sound of the car in the distance, it feels too intimate. No, not intimate. Dirty.

"Hear... what?" he asks.

"A car." I frown. Outside, the road is clear. "Maybe it's the interstate."

Nathan shakes his head. "You must have hearing like a bat." He lets out a soft chuckle.

"Maybe I'm imagining it," I murmur. But I don't think I am. The more I think about it, the more I'm convinced that somewhere nearby is a car, and what's more, *it has slowed down.*

Nathan's smile is kind, crinkling the lines around his ice-blue eyes. "I think you're being paranoid."

I slide off his lap. "Do you blame me? This isn't me, you

know. Fucking my boss in his car... it certainly isn't where I saw my life heading."

"Hey," he says softly. "Look at me. I made this decision. You didn't do anything wrong. I'm the one who's married. It's on me."

But I shake my head because I know it isn't just on him. "Where are they?" I rummage around the footwell, searching for my panties.

"Here," he says with a smirk, lifting one finger with my panties dangling from it.

When I go to snatch them, he pulls them back an inch. "Not until you smile. Come on, we can't end it like this."

But I can't fake it. I grab his wrist gently and pry my underwear from his hand. "Thank you for being kind. But I don't feel like smiling right now. Let's just get out of here. Please?"

For an awkward few minutes, we clean up. Nathan grabs us tissues, and he dumps the condom into the cupholder.

I wrinkle my nose. "That's gross."

A flicker of sadness darkens Nathan's eyes. "Being gross seems to be what I do best recently." He sighs. "Look, I can't throw it out the window so this will have to do for now."

As I shove the used tissues into my purse, I have to agree with him. But I sure as hell won't leave any incriminating evidence behind in this car.

"Make sure you get rid of it before your wife finds it." The word *wife* leaves a sour residue, gritty, on my tongue.

He rolls his eyes, avoiding my gaze. "Do you think I'm stupid?"

I turn away from him.

Nathan touches my arm. "I'm sorry about all this," he

whispers. He still sounds hot. His voice makes the hairs stand up on the back of my arm.

"There's nothing to be sorry about." I hike my underwear back up around my waist, where they belong. "I was a willing participant."

When I pull up my shorts, I vow to myself that this will never happen again. This is the line I'm drawing. Everything I did before now, I can put down to weakness. I lost my mom. I felt sad. I needed someone. But this is it. Watching Nathan put that condom into a cupholder makes me realize how disgusting we are.

"We won't do it again," Nathan says as though reading my mind.

"Agreed." I reach out my hand to shake his, like we are conducting some sort of neutral business transaction.

We spend a few minutes driving up the long, isolated road as I stare at Nathan's phone, trying to get a signal. When bars appear in the top corner, I pull up a map, place it on the dashboard, and push the navigation button. When the route appears, I sigh with relief, leaning into the leather back of the seat.

"Things will be different once we get back to the office," Nathan assures me, speeding up.

I give him a questioning glance. "What do you mean?"

"Different like—back to normal," he explains, cutting me a brief look.

I nod, clasping my hands in my lap. "I hope so."

Nathan's eyes roam across me. "We'll pretend like nothing happened."

The slight change in his tone makes my spine straighten. It's not a suggestion—it's an order. On the one hand, I'm relieved he's serious about this never happening again. On the other hand, for the first time since the night in the bar, I have to consider the ramifications this could have on my career.

"Right." I swallow hard.

Nathan's jaw unclenches. His hand cups over mine. "Everything will be okay."

"Well, if we're going to pretend like nothing happened, we should start by having a no-touching rule." I slide my hand out from under his.

He retracts his hand, giving me a cautious smile. "Good idea."

My fingers tap the armrest, and I consider whether I should say more or leave it be. I decide to speak. "Nathan, when you say we'll get back to normal, do you mean that?"

"In what way?"

"In the way that I can keep my job and I don't have to worry about you treating me any... differently... as a boss."

He gives me a sharp glance. "I'm not an asshole, Lucy. You don't have anything to worry about."

I let out a long breath. There's a stretch of silence.

Then Nathan says, "I understand why you had to ask me that question."

And that's that. He turns on the radio to drown out the awkward silence. Soon we're coasting along the interstate. After a while, my eyelids get heavy, and I shut them. I drift into a fretful car-induced sleep. By the time I wake up, the familiar lights of the city wink around me, a much-needed welcome home.

I open the passenger door and cast Nathan a friendly smile. "Thanks for the ride."

"Which ride are you referring to?" Nathan's blue eyes sparkle with mischief.

I shake my head and wag a finger at him. "No, sir. We're back home. That behavior only existed at the retreat."

Nathan straightens his posture and exhales, his face switching to the epitome of professionalism. "You're right. You're welcome for the ride. Enjoy the rest of your day."

"Thank you."

I roll my suitcase to my front door, not bothering to glance back at Nathan. Behind me, I hear his car drive away and smell tires on asphalt. My hand shakes slightly as I insert the key to unlock my condo.

The hallway is too quiet. After several days of being around company almost twenty-four seven, it takes me a moment to adjust to being alone. But at least it's still daytime and the sun filters in through the window, warming everything it touches. I dump the suitcase in the hall, pull off my shoes, and peel away my clothes on the way to the shower. Drawing a line under everything means washing the scent of him off my body.

In the bedroom, I catch a glimpse of my reflection in the mirror. If anyone saw me now, they'd think I hadn't slept for a week. I make a disgusted sound and step into the shower. Nathan is all over me. His cum, his sweat, his cologne. Our sex —the mistakes we made—lingers. I need it gone. I need a clean start. The water scalds my skin, but I let it, lathering up soap and smearing it everywhere until there are tears in my eyes and my skin stings. By the time I get out, my fingertips are like little shriveled prunes.

This place has no life to it. I survey my sad little condo. I have my photos of friends. My picture of me and Mom on vacation. There are boxes of stuff from ex-boyfriends in the closet and bits and pieces of art on the walls, but there's no one here to wrap his arms around me and tell me that everything will be okay. And if there was, it wouldn't be Nathan.

"I need a cat," I say, rubbing my hair vigorously with a towel. Then I put on the radio and turn it up as loud as I dare without pissing off Mrs. Doebler next-door.

Once in my sweats, I pour out a glass of merlot and collapse on the sofa. *See, this isn't so bad. The single life is way better than being someone's mistress.*

Bopping along to Rihanna, I scroll through social media on my phone, trying to catch up with what friends and family have been up to since I've been at the work function. I wish I could tell someone about what happened between me and Nathan, but I promised to keep my lips sealed. I only hope that Nathan will uphold his end of the deal.

Once I get bored with that, I refill my glass of wine and lie back on the couch, slinging a throw blanket over my legs. Fatigue settles over me as I blindly channel hop, landing on the first sitcom rerun I can find.

I'm about twenty minutes into *New Girl* when my phone vibrates. There's a number on the screen that I don't recognize, and in my half-asleep state, I have to squint a couple of times to figure out what's going on. Someone has sent me a text with an image attached. A *stranger* has sent it.

My heart pounds when I open the message. Nothing good comes from an unknown number. The words in bold make my stomach lurch. But the worst part of the message is the image underneath. *This message can't be for me... can it?*

Yes. Of course it is. Because I'm in the picture attached to the message. It's blurry, and it's certainly zoomed in from a distance, but there I am in all my glory. Through a car window, I can see my naked body sitting on Nathan's lap. My bare ass is pressed against the steering wheel. His hands are on my hips, his head thrown back in ecstasy. My top is pulled down, exposing my breasts, and my hair is messy. I'm turned slightly toward the window, my mouth open, probably moaning. All around us are corn fields reflected in the windows.

This photograph makes me feel like I'm on display, and the blanket tumbles to the carpet when I sit up straight. I scan the room, even though there's no evidence anyone is in the apartment. Then it hits me—someone saw us. Someone watched us.

I jump up, hands shaking, and jog over to the curtains, peeking out to check the sidewalk. Dusk paints an indigo hue over my front lawn. The street is empty.

I snap the curtains shut and return to the couch then sink into it to view the message again. The heat of fear pulses through me. My throat tightens. I gulp in a lungful of air and try to calm my heartbeat. Only when I'm relatively calm do I allow myself to read the message one more time.

I WILL RUIN YOUR LIFE, WHORE. UNLESS YOU PAY.

8

I pace my living room, my heart pounding, my pulse throbbing. *What the fuck is going on? Who sent that message? Who took the photos? Oh, God, there's photographic evidence of Nathan cheating on his wife with me. That's bad.*

I pause, taking a big gulp of wine, hoping it'll calm my nerves. Whoever sent the text must know me—or know someone who has my contact information. Otherwise, they wouldn't have access to my phone number. But this unidentified number was not saved in my phone.

Then I have a thought. I grab my phone, copy the number from the text, and put it through Google. Nothing comes up. They know me, but I have no way of knowing who they are. The thought is unnerving. Paranoid, I walk over to the window and peel back the curtain. As always, there's no one there. It's pitch-black outside. A shiver runs down my spine.

I move away from the window and continue to the back of the condo, switching on every light as I move. Then I sit on the edge of my bed. I stand up and pace again. This is surreal, but now I need to decide whether to message this person back. If I ignore it, I don't know what will happen next. If I respond, perhaps I can talk some sense into the person and get a better idea of what they want from me.

Carving out some sort of plan eases a bit of the panic, but my fingers hover over my phone, trembling. Snatching it up, I unlock the screen, scroll through to the messages, and read it one more time.

I WILL RUIN YOUR LIFE, WHORE. UNLESS YOU PAY.

I drop the phone. Pay what—money? How much? I'm not rich. Why does this person want to target me?

A film of sweat beads on the nape of my neck and collects on my lower back, making my shirt stick to my skin. The back of my hair feels damp, so I twist it into a messy bun to get some of the heaviness off my shoulders. My leg bounces against the bed. I snatch up the phone and tap my reply.

Who is this? I stare at the words on my phone screen then shake my head and press the backspace to delete them. There's no way they will answer that question, so it's a waste of a text message. I blink at the empty space.

What do you want? I type out and send that question instead.

Sitting on the bed is no longer an option. My body wants to move. I open my fridge door and pluck out a water bottle, twist the cap off, and glug down half the container before wiping the dribble off my lips with the back of my hand.

I check my phone. Nothing. I put the water bottle back. To do something with my hands, I begin emptying the dishwasher. I'm partway through placing cutlery in the drawer when a sound stops me in my tracks.

Ping.

My breath comes out in a short, sharp gasp. This is it. I take a cautious step toward the table and retrieve my phone.

$20,000.

I almost laugh. Are they serious? I live in a condo and drive a Kia.

I don't have that kind of money. Who is this? I write, almost annoyed now.

Two ticks tell me the cretin has read the message, but yet again, they keep me hanging. Frustrated, I leave the phone on the table and carry on with my task, banging pots and pans, slamming cupboards. The response comes through about five minutes later in a quiet moment, making me jump out of my skin. I snatch my phone.

Ask your boyfriend.

Pinching my lips together, I type out a hasty response and click Send.

I don't have a boyfriend.

The response is almost instant this time. **And I don't have time for games. If you can't afford it, go to Nathan. Ask him for the money.**

"Oh, sure," I say to nobody. "It's *that* simple. I'll just ask my boss for 20K. What the fuck." I run my hands through my hair. Nathan is not going to be happy about this, but he deserves to know.

After a moment, I dial Nathan's number and place the phone to my ear. He answers with a hesitant whisper. "Lucy? Why are you calling me? I'm at home with my family."

I swallow down my pride, blurting, "We have a problem."

There's a pause before he says, "Hang on a second." I hear footsteps on his end, a door closing. When he speaks again, it's in a normal voice. "Okay, I went outside. What's going on?"

"I received a series of really weird text messages."

"From whom?" His voice is curious but not suspicious, reassuring me that he's not in on whatever this is. I can only hope it's a prank, but I have to treat it as a real threat until I know for sure.

"I don't know."

"All right..."

"It was from a number I don't recognize. They want money. Lots of it."

"Money... for what?"

"They took a picture of us, Nathan." I choke back a nervous sob. Panic thunders through me. "Having sex in your car."

He sighs. "Back up," he says, his voice flattening. He sounds tired. "What are you talking about? You're scaring me."

"*You're* scared? You're not the one being harassed by a mystery person."

"Do you need help? Are you safe?"

I look around my empty kitchen and dare a glance out the window above the sink. There's no action going on in my backyard that I see—no shadows lurking, no movement. Aside from my shallow breathing, I can't hear a thing. It's almost eerily quiet.

"I don't know, Nathan." My voice is shrill. "I'm freaking out."

"All right, just try not to send yourself into a spiral." His voice is soothing enough to knock my prickling fear down a peg.

"It's pretty damn hard not to spiral when there's some sicko out there demanding money and making threats."

"What's the threat?" Nathan asks, his voice clipping on the last word.

"The *money*, remember?"

Nathan hisses out a long breath through the phone. "How much money?"

"Twenty thousand dollars." I enunciate every syllable to make sure he's listening.

"I don't have that kind of money," Nathan says, his teeth gritting.

"Neither do I. They told me to ask you." Another roar of panic splits inside me.

"You said they sent an incriminating picture?"

"If you consider me sitting naked on your lap in your car pulled off to the side of the road incriminating, then yes."

Nathan blows another noisy breath into the phone's receiver. "Shit. Who the hell knew we were out there? Were we being followed?"

"Your guess is as good as mine."

He pauses. "Do you think we were followed? I just... this makes no sense. Did you tell anyone at the retreat about us?"

"No. None of them had a clue. I promise." I rub my temple, thinking. "I don't know how we could have been followed without seeing someone around. We were lost in the middle of nowhere. And how could they even know we were going to... you know. It doesn't make sense."

"You're right."

I sigh. "But I did hear a car. Maybe... maybe someone from the retreat took the same route as us, but we didn't notice them because we were... distracted. And then maybe they grasped this opportunity to mess with us."

"That makes sense. Which one of them could do this? Chet?"

"I don't know. I'll send you the photo now—"

"No, wait. Don't send me the photo."

"Why not?"

When he answers, it's through gritted teeth. "I don't want that evidence on my *phone*. I'm *married*."

"Oh, so it's going to be up to *me* to figure this out on my own, then?" My fingers tighten around my phone.

"I didn't say that." Nathan backpedals. "Just—just let me *think* a minute."

The line goes quiet between us, but the air is heavy.

"I'll look at the photo when we get back to work, and then we'll figure out what to do, but I don't have that kind of money, Lucy. What exactly did the message say?"

I don't want to tell him that the sender called me a whore, so I leave that part out. "That they'd ruin my life unless I pay them twenty thousand dollars."

"And what was the number?"

I read it out painstakingly slowly.

"It doesn't sound familiar," he says, "but I've punched it into my keypad. I'll compare it to the numbers stored in my phone to see if anything adds up."

"Okay. That's a start. Thank you." Relief floods through me. At least Nathan is helping.

I hear a muffled voice on the other end, then Nathan calls out, "Coming, honey. No, it's fine, just work. I'll be right in." His voice is hushed as he comes back to me. "Listen, Lucy, I'm really sorry you are dealing with this tonight, but I have to go. I don't need my wife getting suspicious on top of everything else."

"It's okay, I understand," I say, biting back resentment.

"Call me if they contact you again. Or text me. My wife

doesn't check my phone, luckily, and I don't want to give her any reason to either."

"Okay, I will." I stumble on the words, but I get them out.

"And, Lucy?"

"Yeah?"

"Make sure all your doors are locked tight tonight. I'll see you at work."

9

Standing in my office cubicle, I have a decent vantage point across the open-plan space. White rectangular desks break up the long gray room. It's oddly quiet, with the occasional squeak from Vivian's chair. But as I regard my coworkers, I feel like I'm on display now that my world has been upended.

Aiming to be inconspicuous, I sip coffee from my travel mug and scan the office for anything out of the ordinary. Then I push my arms behind my back as though stretching out my muscles. Nothing is happening, and no one is paying any attention to me.

Always a stickler for routine, Vivian is already planted behind her desk, her eyes fixed on her computer screen, fingers clicking away at her keyboard. She stays in her lane, doesn't get involved in drama, keeps her head down, and does her work. While Vivian has a sassy side, she's a no-nonsense straight talker, and it would be out of character for her to be involved in something like this. Then again, can I trust anyone right now? I slump back into my seat, pretending to type an email.

There's movement from the top of the room. Janine hurries in, toting huge bags over her shoulders, clutching a to-go coffee. Coming in late is pretty normal for Janine, but she always manages to sneak in while Nathan is preoccupied with something. I've never known her to be reprimanded. Is she someone I should watch out for? Does Janine have a history with feeling like she can get away with anything?

I definitely need to keep an eye on her. Janine can get flirty with some of the men working in the office, eligible or not. This includes Nathan. It wouldn't be a stretch to think she might have a jealous streak along with her propensity for drama. But this is all a little sophisticated for Janine. After all, she did decline a ride from Nathan. She didn't even have a car with her. So it doesn't seem plausible that it would be her who saw us. Then again, I can't rule anyone out.

Janine parks herself at her desk, out of breath. The hum of phones becomes background noise. A knot twists in my stomach. Up until this point, I've trusted the people I've worked with. They've given me no reason not to.

The realization that it *has* to be one of these people is like a stake through my heart. Who else would be in that area and have access to my information? My phone number is in the employee system, so it wouldn't be hard to find. We have to have our numbers listed for emergency purposes.

It wouldn't be hard to leave right now. All I have to do is stand up and walk fifteen feet until I'm out of this building. But the picture would still be there. The threat would still hang over my head.

"Hey, girl."

Janine's sudden presence startles me.

I clutch a palm to my chest. "Holy crap. Are you barefoot or something?"

She lifts a stockinged foot. "I thought I'd break in some new shoes, but they're killing my feet, and it's not even ten. I left them by my desk." She leans in, scrutinizing my face. Her heady, floral perfume gives me an instant headache. "You look like you had a rough weekend."

She's not wrong. I spent most of it in bed with the curtains shut, too afraid to leave the house and wishing I had a guard dog.

But Janine gets nothing but my poker face. "I'm fine. I had a bit of a cold coming back from the work retreat. I'm over it now, though."

Janine stares at me over the rim of her coffee, unconvinced. "Are you sure?"

"Yes."

"Oh, well, *I* had a great weekend," she says, clearly wanting me to ask about it.

I swallow hard, pushing my hands behind my back so she won't see my fingers shaking. Thank goodness she can't hear the thundering of my pulse.

"Oh, you went to visit your friend, right?" I try to keep my tone casual, but it's uneven, betraying me.

Janine props her shoulder against the gray wall of my cubicle and yawns. Her expression is absentminded, but I don't let down my guard.

"Yeah, we had the *best* time." She pauses to wink. "If you know what I mean."

"I think the Post-its on my desk know what you mean." I hold one up on my finger, waggling it.

Janine's laughter flutters through the air. She swats at my arm. "Girl, you are funny. Anyway, I have a ton of emails to go through this morning. Although I wish I could ignore them all. Am I right?"

She waits for me to empathize. I paint on a friendly smile and give her what she wants to hear. "Tell me about it."

"See ya later." Janine blows me a kiss and struts away, her black hair bouncing off her shoulders.

I settle into my chair, wishing I could melt into the floor, and wondering when I can safely go to see Nathan. Carrying this fear alone is eating away at me.

My desk phone rings, and I snatch it too fast. "Hello?"

"Come to my office, please." It's Nathan.

"Okay. I'll be there in a sec."

I thought I'd feel relief, but dread drenches me from head to toe. Sure, having someone there to help is a good thing, but I don't know for sure that Nathan *will* help. Convinced that everyone can tell I'm walking differently, I put too much spring in my step. And then I go the opposite way and trudge along the carpet. Finally, I reach Nathan's office and stand awkwardly in the doorway.

If the blackmail bothers him, it doesn't show. While I sweat through my shirt, Nathan appears as effortlessly attractive as always. Sunlight streams in over his face, enhancing his jawline. But this time, I don't go weak at the knees. I know all of that is over now. The sight of Nathan brings me nothing but shame and concern.

"You wanted to see me?" I ask.

"Yes, thank you for coming in." Nathan clears his throat and adjusts his sky blue tie.

I smile. "I work here."

"Well, to my office, then," Nathan corrects, his expression platonic and emotionless.

"Right." I fold my arms. "What do you need?"

Nathan glances over my shoulder. "Let's meet later at that café down the street. You know the one?"

"*Bread and Butter*?"

Nathan nods. "Yes."

I sigh and rake a hand through my hair, relenting. "What time?"

"Twelve thirty. I have meetings until then."

"I'll be there."

"Try to grab a booth in the back if you get there before me," Nathan says as I turn to leave.

I bristle at his short tone but don't give him the satisfaction of seeing it on my face. "Will do," I say without looking back at him.

⁓

I get to the café first and find a booth in the back, as Nathan requested. Caffeine seems like a bad idea considering this anxiety-inducing situation, so I order a mint tea. Before Nathan arrives, I scan the other café patrons, searching for anything unusual.

There's a man sipping coffee, his eyes glued to his laptop. At another booth, a mother with tired eyes scolds her unruly toddler after he tosses a muffin at his sister. Thank God for that kid, because I actually stifle a giggle and my leg stops bouncing up and down beneath the table.

The café door opens, and Nathan strides in. There's no trace of humor on his face, and the sight of him makes my body tense. I lift a hand in greeting, and he nods, his lips set in a grim line. Everything about him says he does not want to be here, and I try not to take it personally. After all, I don't want to be here either. I don't want to be in the middle of this shit show.

He cuts one glance over his shoulder and slides into the booth. "Have you been waiting long?" He looks around, his expression agitated.

I shake my head. "A few minutes or so."

He blows out a sharp breath. "Okay, good."

I study him. "Why did you want to meet up in public like this?"

Nathan frowns. "Well, we aren't doing anything wrong. We're coworkers having lunch. That's normal. If we act like we have nothing to hide, then people will believe it."

He's right, but the unsettled feeling still rattles around inside my head. *Someone* knows we have something to hide, and they are trying to bring it to the surface. Nathan orders a coffee and a blueberry scone. I don't order anything. My stomach continues to churn.

"Also, if we're right, and someone from the office sent you the threat, how do we know they won't also listen in on our conversations?"

"Good point." I run a finger around the rim of my mug.

Nathan places his hands in his lap, leaning forward. "Have you gotten any new messages?"

"No, just the one."

His face relaxes slightly. "Well, maybe that's a good thing."

"But I still have to come up with twenty thousand dollars," I remind him.

Nathan drums his fingers on the surface of the table and studies his lap before lifting his gaze to me. "Can I see the message? And the photo?"

I pull it up on my screen and slide my phone across the table for him to scrutinize.

"It's definitely us." He pushes the phone back to me, frowning.

"You don't recognize the number, do you?"

He shakes his head. "I don't."

I search his expression for lies, but he seems exactly like someone who has been caught cheating and is now being blackmailed. I don't see a trace of anything else.

He crosses his arms, his knee bouncing under the table. "Well, if they haven't contacted you again, maybe you're in the clear."

I lean forward, my eyes wide. "Are you kidding? They named you."

Nathan's cheeks pale, and he shifts his gaze away as if it physically hurts him to look at me.

"Listen, Nathan, we have to take this seriously," I hiss. "They want a lot of money that I don't have."

Nathan scratches his chin, thinking. "Well, we just have to wait and see what they say next—*if* they even try to contact you again."

"Easy for you to say. You're not the one who got the text."

"But it still involves me. Like you said, they used my name." Nathan stumbles over the words.

"What if they up the ante?" I let my derailing thoughts run away with me as I speak. "What if they show up at my house?"

Nathan's eyes lock with mine. There's sympathy in them. Pity perhaps. "Try not to think in a fatalist way like that. Do your best to take it one minute at a time. Right now, for all you know, they only have your number. Maybe they don't know where you live."

I sink into the pleather seat and let out a slow exhalation. "I hope you're right."

"You said you responded to them last night, but try not to engage anymore. Especially if they aren't going out of their way to contact you." He pats me on the arm. "Don't worry, Luce. This will all blow over. I'm sure of it."

I yank my arm away. There's much more I want to say, but I don't. It's clear Nathan isn't going to help me. Whatever happens next, I'm going to have to deal with it alone.

10

The week goes by in a blur. For the first three days, every time my phone pings, my body tenses.

"Hey, Jumpin' Jack Flash," Chet says over my cubicle wall, grinning. "Maybe put that thing on silent."

Vivian lets out a snort.

"What's wrong, anyway?" he asks. "You've been acting weird all week."

"It's personal," I say.

He shrugs. "All right. Well, if you need anything..."

I glance at Vivian, who is back to her work. Janine is on the phone. Nathan is in his office. Am I the only one who finds that interaction weird—Chet being *nice*? That's suspicious.

By Friday, I've heard nothing from the blackmailer, and I feel somewhat normal again. Meetings no longer make me want to sink into a black hole and never come out. Nathan and I have reached a tentative balance when it comes to how we talk to each other at work. At the end of the week, we say a quick goodbye and enter separate cars.

Is it over? Can I go back to normal now? With every ion of my being, I hope so.

On Sunday night, I'm in my kitchen, setting my coffee maker for the morning, getting things prepared for the work week ahead. I have Kendrick Lamar on in the background, drowning out the silence, as I move around the kitchen, in my element.

When the album ends, I stop. For the first time since the retreat ended, I haven't thought about Nathan or the threatening text. Dread seeps over me. When I pick up my phone, I'm convinced that it's about to happen again. But the only notification on my screen is for a spam email. Then I notice it's nearly eleven and head through the condo to my bedroom.

One of the perks of being single is not worrying what you wear at night. Tonight, it's my vintage *Buffy the Vampire Slayer* shirt with bright-pink shorts. I pile my hair atop my head, fix it with a scrunchie, and climb into bed.

And then it happens. *Ping.*

A cold fist seizes my heart. The sight of my pale, trembling fingers alarm me as I reach for the phone. There's a text-message notification on the screen.

No. No, no, no, no. I just got back to normal. I found myself again amid the fear and anxiety of last week.

One glance confirms that it's the same number as before. I swipe the phone open.

Where's my 20K?

I close my eyes, squeeze them tight, and open them again. Part of me thinks I am dreaming. Nope, this is real. And there's an attachment to the message. *Fuck. What now?*

The photo is clearer this time. It's not as zoomed in or pixilated, but it's just as incriminating, if not more so because both of our faces are visible. There we are, Nathan and I, sitting in the booth at *Bread and Butter*. I lean into him, my cheeks blotchy and red. God, Janine was right, I did look awful last week. Nathan's body is tense, his eyes angled down at his hands on the table. There's nothing wrong with us sitting in the café together, but whoever sent this message also stalked us.

Stalked.

I didn't want it to be true, but this confirms my worst fears. Whoever wants the money has followed us at least twice. That means whenever I go anywhere, someone is watching me. My eyes trail over to the curtains, checking for any gaps within the fabric. There are none. But I still can't stop myself from picturing a face outside the window. Watching. Waiting. Gooseflesh erupts over my arms. My scalp prickles.

I regard the photograph one more time, zooming in for clues. From the angle and the slight distortion across the picture, it seems as though they took the photo from outside the café. I guess that means they didn't come too close. And it definitely means they didn't overhear our conversation. But none of that gives me much comfort.

Needing to do something, I get out of bed, pull on a pair of slippers, and trek through the rooms, switching on every single light. I would put the floodlights on if it wouldn't piss off Mrs. Doebler.

Back in bed, I watch the ceiling-fan blades whirl. My thoughts spin. *Why is this person texting me and not Nathan? Surely, he's the one with the money. He's a manager after all. I mean, neither of us is rich, but he's slightly wealthier.*

I'm easier, I decide. Young, female, single. I'm easier to threaten, and this piece of shit knows that. The thought makes me angry. I hold onto that sensation. When I view the text message one more time, I picture them laughing at me, thinking I'm in my house, sobbing my eyes out. But I'm not. I'm furious.

"I need to talk to you." I march into Nathan's office, uninvited, at seven in the morning, well before anyone else is scheduled to work.

Nathan sits behind his desk exactly where I expect him to be. He's the team manager, overseeing more than a dozen employees. He has a lot of responsibilities, and he's always been a morning person. Unless he has a prior appointment, he arrives to the office like clockwork every day at seven a.m.

Nathan lifts his head. His brow furrows, and I think he's about to yell at me. Then he gets to his feet and steps around the desk.

"Has something happened?"

I shove my phone at him, waving the picture in his face. "So much for ignoring them."

He grabs the phone, his hands as hungry as they were in that hotel room. He fingers the screen, zooming in on our faces. "What the hell? Who...?"

"Imagine getting that at eleven at night, and you'll feel what I felt. Someone is watching us. And they aren't backing down."

He puts the phone on his desk and paces his office. I wait, giving him time to process this new turn of events. A moment later, he tugs at his tie, pulling it from around his neck, and throws it onto his office chair.

"You need to block this number and forget about it," he

says, loosening the top button on his shirt. "What are they going to do?"

"Tell your wife?" I suggest.

He swallows, and his Adam's apple dips and bobs. "They won't. It's all a bluff, Lucy."

"We should go to the police. This is out of control now. Whoever this is has followed us twice. I don't feel safe at home. Do you feel safe?"

"I don't feel unsafe." He shrugs. "They'd be a terrible blackmailer if they killed their only chance at getting the money." Nathan glances at his door, walks over to the entrance, checks the office for anyone listening, then closes it and moves over to his desk.

"I don't like this. It's easy for you to say you're safe. I live alone, remember? They're targeting me for a reason. I'm the weakest. I mean... they could do something to me to get to you." I ball my hands into fists. "Nathan, I need to go to the police. I can't live like this. I can't simply block the number and move on. At the very least, we need to find out who is sending these texts—get an IP address or something."

"Do I look like a cell phone hacker to you?" Nathan barks.

I lift my hands, placating him. "I'm just trying to figure this out. I'm not your enemy here."

At first, I think he's going to soften. But then he takes a step closer so that I can smell the wood musk of his cologne. "Let's get to the root of that, shall we?"

I swallow hard. "The root of what?"

"Exactly who your enemies are." His gaze burns into me as if he's trying to search my soul.

"I don't *have* any enemies, Nathan. What about you?"

His eyes flick away. "I don't have any either."

I move to the side so that we're face-to-face. "You're

married, Nathan. And exactly how many times have you cheated on her?"

He grits his teeth, hissing. "Just those two times with you. I told you that."

"Well, what if she found out?"

"How could my wife know I'd screw someone in my car?"

"Maybe she had you followed."

He shakes his head. "No. She knows nothing."

"How can you be sure?"

"Because I know her. I know her better than you, anyway. For all I know, there could be someone in your past. Are you hiding anything?"

"I'm hiding nothing." My throat goes dry under his scrutiny. *Am I being truthful? Is there something I'm neglecting?* "Look," I say, backpedaling, trying to keep my voice steady and low. "It could be anyone. It could be someone we don't even realize. A person in our past life we aren't even thinking about."

"Well, it's not my wife, so you can stop your detective work right there," Nathan snaps, turning his back to me again, his hands planted on his hips.

"All right, fine. Well, if you don't have any other suggestions or solutions—"

"I don't. And please block the number. I don't have time to deal with this anymore."

"Fine, Nathan. I'll block the number. If you want to ignore this until it's too late, then that's what we'll do. But you can't say I didn't warn you." I slam the door so hard the walls vibrate.

11

Chet rests a hip against my desk and grins. "Good morning, Lucy."

Three days of blissful silence have passed. No texts. No threats. Only work to deal with, and it's been particularly busy in the office.

I match Chet's sickly sarcastic tone. "Hey, Chet."

"I'm so glad we're teaming up. I finally get to spend some time with the quietest chick in the office."

I roll my eyes. "You do realize that you're going to end up fired for sexual harassment before you can take Nathan's job, don't you?"

"The rumors are cruel, my dearest friend." He places a hand on his heart. "I am but a humble..."

I snort.

He eyeballs me. "A humble young man aiming to carve his way through this muddy hell we call life. Can't a man have a bit of fun these d—"

"Chet," I say. "Did you book the meeting room?"

"Yes, my sweet." He winks. "Come this way."

"Okay, you need to knock it off because I'm already losing the will to live." I stand up from my desk and follow him through the office.

Vivian glances up and smiles then returns to her work. Janine bites down on a pen and stares at her computer screen. Something seems to be bothering her. Perhaps it's Nathan's schedule.

It's strange how the office is already seemingly normal again. I actually think that the blackmailer isn't anyone here after all. Maybe that's wishful thinking.

We head through to the meeting room, and Chet shuts the door behind us. I'm not thrilled about having to work with him, but we got this last-minute proposal to land a new client, and it's a big one—Davina Clothing. They're a huge international corporation. Snagging them as a client would be a monumental step up for my career—and my paycheck. Chet is the more experienced marketer, and if I want to learn the ropes and climb the corporate ladder, I'm going to have to put my disdain for him aside.

As I'm about to set down my laptop, Chet stares at his phone and lets out a curse. "We're going to have to go to the conference room, Luce."

"Wait, what?"

"Yeah, so there's been a change of plans." Chet grabs his laptop and a folder and heads for the door. "The CEO of Davina is coming in with her assistant, and we have to be ready to make this deal today." He pauses and eyes me up and down as if sizing me up, his brows quirking. "Are you ready?"

I paint on a superficial smile and pat my laptop. Chet won't see *me break* a sweat, even if I'm cracking under the surface. "All set."

"Good." The grin is back.

Even on the wrong foot, he manages to stay cocky. Unfortunately, in this business, arrogance is an asset—clients respond to confidence. But I'm pretty certain one day Chet is going to go too far.

When we get to the conference room, which is bigger than the tiny meeting room we started in, he closes the door behind us again. A thought flashes through my mind. *Is this a mind game? Did he set up this switching of rooms and sudden appearance from the potential client? Is he trying to wrong-foot me?*

I start setting up the screen and clear my throat. "So, did you get the email?"

"Yep. Right before we came here." His eyes narrow. "You saw me get the email."

"I know."

I walk back over to the table and roll my fingers over my laptop mouse to wake up the screen. Chet's warm coffee breath tickles my neck as he hovers over my shoulder.

"Wow, you've put a lot of thought into this." He sounds earnestly impressed, which surprises me and gives me a little zing of confidence.

I glance at him over my shoulder, wishing he'd sit down and stop loitering. "Thanks. I didn't have a lot of time, but I did my best."

"You did great." Chet points to a few topics for discussion on how to steer the marketing that I've bulleted on the program. "This one especially."

"I hope they like it."

"I don't see why they wouldn't," Chet says, finally sitting down next to me, his arm brushing mine.

Our eyes lock, and I wonder whether he slyly made that skin contact on purpose. His expression is hard to read. I guess it's part of his persona. One moment, he cracks an inappropriate joke, and the next, he's sincere.

"Can you check the projector?" I ask. "I plugged it in, but it's always been a bit iffy with me."

"I'll handle it," Chet says, waking his laptop to plug it into the projector.

I can't help but notice his eyes keep skating between me and his screen, a curious gleam adding to his peculiar behavior. *Is he interested in me, or is it something darker than that? What hides beneath his jokey surface—a blackmailer?*

His voice slices through my deep thoughts. "It looks like I'm going to end up with an excellent partner to lock in this deal after all." The zesty twinkle in his eyes sparks across the space between us.

"Careful, Chet. People might start to think you're nice."

He laughs. "Maybe I am."

I'm not sure what alternate reality I'm living in where Chet is a nice person. Unless the nice behavior is a front to distract me from him being the blackmailer.

He rubs his fingertips across his square jaw, his attention invested in the computer program. His flirting seems too innocent, or too eager, to make me believe that he has anything to do with the strange text messages. He's not giving off any suspicious vibes. It doesn't seem like he's trying to study my behavior to see if *I'm* suspicious about *him.* I decide not to rule him out, but alarm bells aren't ringing inside my head either.

These thoughts do me no good. I shut them down before they spiral. The only thing that matters right now is the client.

The door bursts open. Isabelle Davina marches in, her perfume immediately choking the room. She's wearing a navy silk dress, her cheeks rosy with rouge and wearing candy-apple-red lipstick. Her blond hair is pulled up in an impeccable bun. Diamonds dangle from her earlobes and sparkle on her fingers. Her eyes are steely blue but stormy.

Behind her shuffles in Monica, the building receptionist. She gives an apologetic grimace, her eyes skirting between me and Chet as she mouths, "I'm sorry, she whisked right past me."

Isabelle is the heir to the clothing line created by her father. I see the resemblance in those penetrating eyes as her commanding stare holds conference with my own. This is not going to be an easy pitch.

"You are Lucy Croft?" Isabelle asks.

I set my shoulders straight and nod, feeling everyone's gaze flick to my direction.

Isabelle shoves her expensive designer tote into a chair and whips out her phone. She jabs her perfectly manicured fingers onto the screen and pushes the phone into my face.

"Care to explain *this*? And I get a notification about this only *minutes* before our meeting is set to commence? And you want *my* business?"

I shake my head, reeling. *What is this crazy woman talking about?* I try to focus my eyes on the screen, but the panic pounding through my head has my vision blurring.

"I'm sorry, what?" I stammer.

Chet steps forward, his eyebrows knitting with concern. "Is there... a problem?"

Isabelle juts out one hip and plants a hand on it before tossing me an incriminating leer. "You tell me."

I swallow down the knot of panic in my throat and finally scrutinize the screen. What I see shocks me. My own name, my own picture, plastered all over every social media outlet

Isabelle has stored. She scrolls to one after the other. Her cheeks are blotched red, and her shoulders rise and fall with rapid anger.

I shake my head. "There must be some mistake. I didn't write or say any of this."

Isabelle narrows her eyes with distrust. She's quiet, but I can still hear her breathing fast. "You didn't start *false* rumors that our fashion company uses slave labor in impoverished countries?"

My throat is scratchy, like I drank hot gasoline. "I did not."

Isabelle moves the phone to her face, studies it, then shoves it toward me. "You are Lucy Croft, are you not?"

"Y-Yes," I stammer.

Beside me, Chet shifts his weight from hip to hip.

"This is your picture, is it not?" Isabelle blinks at me.

"Yes, but I—"

"This is all the confirmation I need," she snaps. "This meeting is officially over. We will not be doing business with your firm after all."

Before she can give either me or Chet a chance to explain, Isabelle spins on a defiant heel and struts from the room. The walls close in on me. My skin chills. When I blink, I see the afterimage of my face on those social media posts.

What the hell just happened?

I thought, for the briefest of moments, that Nathan might have been right about blocking the blackmailer. I dared to think that maybe I could move on with my life. But it's clear, I cannot. They've raised the stakes. My blackmailer has twisted this nightmare, and now they're ready to hammer in every nail of my coffin until I'm buried alive.

12

Nathan takes a sip of water. It's his third in thirty seconds. He sets the glass back down on the coaster and wipes his mouth.

"Can you please not do that?" I cut him an irked glance.

"Do what?"

"Slurp water," I snap. "I can't think with you drinking all the time."

Nathan's jaw flexes, and he looks away, miffed. "I'm sorry, Lucy. It's just that I didn't think I would have to attend a disciplinary meeting in the middle of my already packed-to-the-gills schedule."

"It's not my fault." My ego is bruised, and it comes through in my voice. "I didn't want to block the blackmailer. It escalated everything, and *that's* why I'm here. And why you're here. Blame your own shitty advice."

Nathan's eyes pan to mine. His jaw is still locked tight. "Yeah, well, if you hadn't thrown yourself at me in a bar, we wouldn't have been blackmailed."

"Are you fucking *insane*?" Adrenaline courses through my

veins, making me feel like I'm lit up like a power grid. I glare at him. "How dare you say that to me? You sure weren't whistling that tune while you had my pants pulled down around my ankles."

He leans forward as if he's afraid of being overheard, but we're the only ones in the room. Then he sighs. "I'm sorry. I'm wound up tight, and I'm taking it out on you. Things aren't great at home. Then there's all this going on at work. And I know you're stressed, too. This is a real bummer."

"A bummer? It's more than that for me. This job is all I have."

And then it hits me. What if Nathan doesn't believe the person who wrote those posts is the blackmailer? I'll be forced to be my own advocate, which will be extremely challenging, because it will be my word against everyone else's. How can I prove that I didn't set up those social media accounts when my name and picture are plastered all over them?

Nathan reaches for the water again but stops before his fingers touch the glass. "Well, I think we've both learned a lesson about restraint during all of this. Honestly, Lucy, if this job is all you have, why did you sleep with your boss?"

I snap my head back as if he just slapped me in the face. "Why did you sleep with your younger employee? Because that's sexual harassment, isn't it?"

Nathan's eyes widen with paranoia, and he glances over his shoulder, his expression marked with apprehension. "Can you please not talk about that here?"

"Where else can we talk about it? It seems that whoever is out to get us is always one step ahead, knowing everywhere we go, everything we do."

"Whoever is out to get *you*," he corrects. "And I hardly

think there is someone following us around the clock. You're exaggerating."

"How do you know that?"

Nathan pauses, scratching the hairline at the nape of his neck. His eyes are everywhere, landing at different places around the room but never holding a spot for longer than a few seconds.

"Because I'm perceptive," he explains. "I would've noticed if someone were watching me like a hawk."

I lean back in my chair and fold my arms. "You sure didn't seem too acutely aware of your surroundings while I was on your lap in the car."

Nathan flinches, briefly shutting his eyes. "Let's stop. We need to talk about how to keep you from losing your job."

"Then back me up," I hiss right as the door opens.

Nathan rolls his chair away from me so fast, I wonder if he'll get whiplash. I understand, though. I don't want to raise any extra suspicion. I'm in hot water enough as it is.

Nathan's boss, Lucas Weathers, enters the room. He has a thick neck, a red face, and pale-gray eyes that stare right through me. He sits down across from me and Nathan with a grunt. I clasp my hands in my lap and sit up straight. Nathan clears his throat, adjusts his tie, and makes sure his chair is a safe distance from mine, leaving a large gap between us.

I hold my breath, not daring to release it until Lucas speaks. His voice is flat, and his eyes are hollow, but when they reach mine, I note the flicker of disapproval staring back at me. I swallow hard and wait to hear my fate.

"This Davina client is very upset about the posts to your social media accounts," Lucas says, keeping his eyes locked on me.

"I understand they would be. However, there's been a misunderstanding," I say.

Lucas quirks one eyebrow. "What kind of misunderstanding?"

"Those aren't my social media accounts. They're fake. Someone set me up."

Lucas skirts his eyes to Nathan, waiting for confirmation.

"She says they aren't hers." Nathan shrugs. "She's never given us a problem before. I have no reason not to believe her."

It's a lukewarm response but seems appropriate for the kind of man I'm learning Nathan is—someone who always puts himself first. From a career perspective, I can see where Nathan is coming from. He has his own interests to protect and a reputation to uphold, and what does it matter to him what happens to me? I'm not his wife or his girlfriend. I'm the idiot who thought with her sexual appetite instead of with her brain.

"They *aren't* mine." I pull out my phone, scrolling to my real social media pages, and swipe them in front of Lucas so he can see the proof. "See? These were created over ten years ago. This one, seven. There's not one mention of Davina in all the posts I've made." I move my phone back to my lap and scroll to the fake accounts. "Look at these. You can see this one was created last week. It's the one that's posting all the problems and lies about the client."

Lucas exchanges a wary look with Nathan. My heart hammers with dread, but if he doesn't fire me immediately and gives me a chance to explain myself, maybe my odds of being able to stay employed with this company are better than I thought.

Lucas shifts his weight in the chair and rests his hands on

the table. "Yes, but *you* could have very well created those fake accounts just to post those things."

"Why would I risk my career like that?"

"Perhaps you have some sort of belief... or cause... that you find more important than your job," Lucas suggests, his bushy eyebrows lifting.

"Then I wouldn't be here," I say. "I wouldn't fight to stay at this company. And I wouldn't have set up a presentation that even Chet remarked was good. I wouldn't have done any of those things. I would've posted those rumors and never bothered coming into the office."

I glance at Nathan, hoping he'd back up the logic, but he remains silent. Lucas, however, seems to listen.

"The thing I don't understand," Lucas says, "is why this has been done in your name. Why you? Why not an anonymous account?"

"I guess me being in marketing makes it seem more legit," I offer, though I feel the argument is weak.

He nods. "Perhaps. Either that, or someone doesn't like you very much."

"We have no proof either way," Nathan adds, but I don't know if it will help or hurt my case.

"Not without an IP address," I add to make myself look like I know what I'm talking about and to make them consider that there are other ways to prove my innocence in all this. "I'm as surprised as you are. I swear it. And honestly, Isabelle Davina is terrifying. Why would I go into the conference room and subject myself to that buzzsaw of a woman if *I* was the person who posted the rumors? I'd want to avoid her at all costs, wouldn't I?"

Lucas pinches the bridge of his nose with his thumb and index finger and snaps his eyes closed. "I really don't have time to deal with this. We need to fix it. Damage control. Douse the fire." He opens his eyes. "Consider this a verbal warning. You need to get the accounts taken down immediately. You have twenty-four hours."

He stands. Nathan snaps to attention, following him out and offering apologies and promises I'm not sure he can fulfill. I rise to my feet, but my knees buckle, and my legs feel like they're made of jelly. I somehow manage to make it to Nathan's office. His door is closed. I knock but don't wait to get an approval before stumbling through the door. Nathan's head jerks up from his computer when I enter. I close the door behind me and lock it.

"Thanks for sticking your neck out for me back there," I tell him, making sure he catches the sarcasm in my voice.

He sighs, rolling his eyes. "Lucy, listen—"

I approach his desk, pointing an accusatory finger an inch from his perfect face. "No, Nathan, *you* listen. I'm tired of being the only one affected by this."

"By what?" He seems flabbergasted, deepening my confusion.

"By whatever this blackmailer is trying to do to us."

"To you."

"Stop saying that!" I bark.

Nathan's shoulders wilt, and his expression drains. "I don't know what else to do."

"Help me, then. Help me figure out who is doing this to me. I know the blackmailer is behind these fake social media accounts."

"But like you said in the meeting, there's no way to prove it."

"How am I supposed to get them taken down if I don't even know where they're originating?" My voice is laced with pleading. I hate myself for sounding so pathetic, but I'm at the end of my rope.

Nathan's eyes don't focus on me. He stares over my shoulder at the wall behind me. "I don't know what to say."

I shake my head. "So, that's it?"

His features soften, his eyes creasing, but he doesn't smile. "At least you didn't get fired."

"I will soon if I can't figure out how to get rid of those accounts."

"I doubt it." Nathan shrugs as if I'm blowing this whole thing out of proportion. "You're an excellent member of our team, and Lucas knows that. You probably just won't get to work on this account."

"Why don't you care about this more?"

His eyes lift to mine. I'm hovering over his desk. He moves his arms out to his sides. "Tell me how to fix it, and I will."

I frown at him. I didn't expect him to say this, which is why I'm unprepared to give him an answer. At that moment, I realize he's right. There's no simple way to get out of this situation. Nathan can't help me. I need to find a way to do it myself. Maybe it's time to put myself first like Nathan is doing.

13

I don't realize I'm grinding my teeth until my jaw starts to ache. Leaning forward, I rest an elbow on my desk and place my head in my hands. Everyone is staring at Vivian and at Lucas Weathers standing by her desk. Why this had to be a spectacle, I don't know.

"Congratulations." Lucas pumps Vivian's hand. "Thanks to your hard work, Isabelle Davina is bringing her clothing line into Cutler-Stewart full-time. And after our first misstep, this is a fantastic achievement. You've earned this, Vivian. Don't let us down."

She beams. I've never seen her so happy. I sit up so I can clap for her. She did do a great job, and even though I can't quell the disappointment, it's still good that the company got a new client. Do I wish it was me? Of course, I do. Part of me wants to disappear into the bathroom and have a good cry. But what good would that do?

A cluster of people gather around Vivian's desk, with Janine at the front. I turn away. Vivian deserves congratulations for putting together a great pitch. I, on the other hand, am not allowed anywhere near Davina Clothing, will not be in the office when she comes in for meetings—at Isabelle's request—and probably won't see a promotion for a very long time. But at least I still have my job.

This is what Mom would do—she'd look on the bright side. She'd find the good bit and tell me to concentrate on that. Dad and I are realists. At least, I was until I slept with my boss. That was the action of a fantasist. But it has brought nothing but grief.

I examine Nathan now, standing behind Vivian's chair, and I can't stand him. When we're together, we do nothing but argue. He hasn't helped or supported me. He's made it abundantly clear that this is my problem and I'm the one who has to deal with it alone.

His only concern is me not going to the police. He's so sure he's not going to be dragged into this and the blackmailer won't get his number and mess with him, too. Is he that cocky, or is there more going on?

And speaking of suspicions, there is Vivian, reaping the rewards of my failure. She's glowing as she celebrates with Janine and the others. She'll probably get a sizable raise, too, along with clout.

These are all major incentives for blackmail. If it was anyone else, I'd be suspicious right away, but with her, it feels off. It's like there's a missing puzzle piece that I still haven't connected yet.

I've never had any run-ins with Vivian. And she's not one to gossip. Whenever something goes on around the office, it's more likely that *Janine* will be the one to chirp the rumors through everybody's ears. But Janine isn't the one climbing up the corporate ladder right now. Vivian is. Maybe that's important.

I give up trying to work and clock out early for lunch. I hope a dose of sugar and caffeine will help snap me out of this funk. But I don't fancy eating out, not with the blackmailer following me, so I grab a large latte and a grilled cheese to bring back to the office.

As I plow out of the elevator, the person waiting almost walks straight into me. I gasp, rolling back on my heels to stop the hot coffee from spilling all over her blouse. I let out a nervous laugh when I see who it is.

"Vivian," I say breathlessly. "I'm sorry, I didn't see you there."

"No problem." Vivian smiles, but her lips are tight as if she's uncomfortable.

Then I realize that I have yet to congratulate her. "Hey. Sorry, I've been busy this morning. I just wanted to say it's great you got the Davina account. I know you'll do great. Good luck."

Vivian barely reacts at first. In fact, she appears almost apologetic, as if she doesn't know what to say to make me feel better. If it's an act, it's a good one.

"Thank you, Lucy. I know this must be tough for you after what happened." She slips her fingers together. "It's a shame it didn't work out for you."

Heat flutters across my face, but Vivian's eyes are kind, not at all condescending or boastful.

"It's okay." I shrug, feigning nonchalance. "I'm sure something else will come along."

Her eyes twinkle as she pushes the down button on the elevator. It lights up the number above the doors, which ding as they open. When she steps inside, I'm relieved I won't have to stand here talking to her.

Before the doors close, she looks me up and down, a mask over her features making it harder for me to gauge what she's thinking. "I'm sure it will, dear. See you later."

The doors shut. She's gone.

That was... weird. She came across as so gracious until the final glance. I go back over our conversation piece by piece. My brain is desperate to pick out anything that doesn't seem right. Maybe she's a better actress than I give her credit for. She is the loner type. Sometimes loners can harbor terrible secrets. Then again, I can't exactly pin the blame on her because she's shy and quiet.

There has to be another explanation. When it comes to Vivian, I don't get the impression she's hiding more depth of personality underneath the layers. Then again, how well can you ever know anyone, much less a coworker who's never been more than an acquaintance?

The thoughts dissipate as I make my way back to my desk. Chet is waiting for me. He points to a paper bag on my desk.

"Don't say I never buy you anything," he says.

I place down my coffee. "Is it safe? There's not rat poison inside, is there?"

He holds up his hands. "Not guilty."

Flashing him a half smile, I open the bag and find a chocolate muffin inside. "Aw. A pity muffin."

"Yep. I made that just for you."

I can't help but laugh. "Thanks."

"Look, I know you didn't make those social media profiles. I don't know who you've pissed off, but they're clearly unhinged. Also, I thought you might think it was me.

But it wasn't. I refused to pitch for Davina again after the way she treated you."

"Well, she was kinda within her rights, considering what she thought I did."

He shrugs. "There are classy ways of dealing with things, and then there's Isabelle Davina. She was *not* classy."

I have to agree with that. "Thank you for this. I needed it."

He nods and walks away. *What timeline am I in? Now Nathan's the douche and Chet's actually nice?*

I get back into my work, the grilled cheese, coffee, and chocolate muffin all going down nicely. But soon, I notice a shadow forming over my computer. When I glance behind me, Nathan is standing there, his eyes wide like a deer trapped in headlights. His face is white as a sheet.

I stand. "What's wrong?"

Nathan reaches into his pocket and pulls out a piece of paper. His eyes roam the empty cubicle space around me. Janine's phone rings. She answers it and chats in her bubbly voice that carries through the maze of desks.

"Oh my gosh, how *are* you, girl? I haven't talked to you in *forever*." Janine's voice zips around us from a few cubicles in front of me. I ignore her and pull my attention to Nathan.

"I got this," he whispers, handing me the folded paper as if we're embroiled in a drug deal.

My heart rate spikes as I take the paper and carefully unfold the creases. Nathan blocks the view of the paper from everyone else in the office.

"It came in my mail this morning," he says. "It wasn't postmarked. It was just tucked under all the other envelopes. I don't think anyone saw it. It was still sealed when I opened it."

His voice is nervous and shaky. A prickling sensation

spreads across my scalp. If Nathan's on edge, then we've got a serious problem.

Scribbled in all capital letters with a permanent black marker are the words:

20K. I'm waiting.

I turn to him. "Welcome to my world."

14

It's like we're being haunted. Some sort of ghoul has latched onto us and won't let go. But the ghoul resembles a friend. It could be any friend—it's impossible to know which one. I can't tell anyone about my ghoul because doing so affects another person, his wife, and his children. Living is lonely because there's no one to turn to.

Nathan is shaken by the note, but the truth is, there's not much we can do about a piece of paper with a threat scribbled on it. On the other hand, it proves one thing: the blackmailer is in the office. We don't talk much after the note. I think he might even be suspicious, as though I'm orchestrating this whole thing to scam money out of him. I suppose it could make sense if I was that kind of person.

And then our attention turns to the Illinois Marketing Awards, or the IMAs, that we have to attend. This year, they'll be hosted at a hotel near Willis Tower, a thirty-mile drive from my condo. Which means I will drive there. I don't want to drink anyway. I need to keep my mind focused.

I'm in the bathroom of the event, listening to muted laughter coming from the crowd. The host is some local comedian that hasn't managed to make me crack a smile. At least, not a genuine smile. I stare at my reflection. For the first time since the retreat, I look good. A color-correcting kit sorted out the dark circles beneath my eyes, and my new red dress is tight in the right places. Annoyingly, the stress has made me drop fifteen pounds. It suits me, but I resent it. Inside, I'm ugly.

I shouldn't be here. I should be filing a police report, ending this once and for all. Yet I'm glammed up, plastering a fake smile on my face. There's an invisible boundary I'm afraid to cross.

The truth is, I'm more than aware of the fact that Nathan's life will be ruined if I go to the police, but I'm not only thinking about him. I'm thinking about me. There's no way I come out of this looking good, and deep down, I'm thoroughly ashamed. Everyone will know I slept with my boss. How could I carry on working at Cutler-Stewart knowing that? Especially after what happened with Davina Clothing.

I wipe my hands on a paper towel and pull the door open. The rush of chatter becomes louder as I return to the table and take my seat next to Angela. She turns to me and smiles, the fine lines wrinkling around her eyes. Of course, I would end up seated next to Nathan's wife, making this situation even more awkward and soul destroying.

"You okay?" she asks.

"Yeah, fine."

We're momentarily distracted by the need to clap. I notice Nathan on Angela's other side, his eyes nervously flitting between us. He's sweating. I spot his handkerchief coming out every so often to mop his face. Hopefully, Angela will put it down to nerves about the award. We got a nod for our social media marketing for a Broadway play. I worked hard on that account, and despite everything, I still care about whether we win.

"Nathan is so nervous," Angela whispers to me. "You seem a little tense, too."

"I guess I am," I say.

She's a beautiful woman. While I'm short and curvy, Angela is built like a runway model, only not as sinewy. Her silky dark hair is curled tonight, and emerald earrings peek out from the waves. Why Nathan would ever want to cheat on her, I have no idea, but here we are.

"Me, too," she confesses. "Only not about the award. I need to talk to you."

"What about?" I ask, breathless.

But she shakes her head, and her eyes turn toward Nathan. We go quiet, focusing on the awards presentation. If I wasn't stressed out before, I am now.

A few minutes later, Nathan is greeted by some executives from another firm. They stand and chat for a while. Then he excuses himself and walks away from the table.

Angela grabs my hand, her fingers clutching mine with surprising force. "Lucy, I'm so worried. Nathan's cheating. I know he is."

"Wh-What?"

"He's not the same. Something is going on. I'm sure of it. And I think you know, too. You do, don't you? Please tell me."

Her dark eyes frighten me. Angela has always been notoriously high-strung. Janine used to joke about how many times a day she'd call the office. And I know it bothers Nathan. He'd given me an insight about that at the retreat.

"I… I don't," I say. "Sorry."

The lie feels oily on my tongue, but what else am I supposed to say?

She lets me go. "Sorry. That was rude. I didn't mean to." She lifts a glass of champagne from the stem and sips it. The drink seems to calm her, but I notice moisture sheens across her eyes. "I need to talk to him about it."

"That's probably for the best," I say, squirming lower in my seat. *Let Nathan deal with it. Let him tell her gently rather than her finding out when the police knock on the front door.* I give Nathan too much credit, though.

I can't help but wonder why she chooses to talk about this with me, especially in a public place with Nathan nearby. From the back of the room, I hear his boisterous laugh. I see him at the bar, talking to associates. It annoys me. He's drinking with friends while I comfort his wife.

Angela's eyes lift and meet with mine. A snide smirk tugs at the edges of her lips. "I must admit, I thought you'd know more."

My fingertip plays with the rim of my soda. "What makes you say that?"

"You're a good listener, Lucy. I figured if my guilty husband confided with someone at work, it would probably be you."

"Oh, he's much closer with Janine and Vivian." I regret the words as soon as they're out of my mouth. She latches onto them immediately.

"Janine? Really?"

"Well, she organizes his calendar. So…"

Angela sips her champagne.

My heart pounds. My back feels sweaty.

Angela waves a hand. "How do I ask my husband if he's a cheater?"

I swallow, and my throat is dry. *Why won't she move on from this conversation?* I sip my soda before answering.

"Just ask him if he's cheating," I suggest.

Angela cuts her eyes to me. Her expression is unreadable, but she searches me for clues, sniffing me out. I know it. Like a hunter seeking its prey.

"And what makes you think that he'd tell me the truth?" she asks.

"I—I don't." I look away.

This is beginning to feel calculated. First, the hand grab, then the confession, and now the focus on what I think and why I might know more. She's sussing me out. And what's worse, I think I'm emanating guilt. How could I not be? I'm not a good liar. I pray for Nathan to return.

"No. I've decided. I'm not confronting him without evidence." Angela glances behind us at the bar, probably checking to see that Nathan isn't on his way back. "Which means I need you to be my eyes and ears in the office. Can you do that?"

Jesus Christ. What am I supposed to say to that? There's only one thing I can say. "I'll try. I think you give me too much credit, though. I'm not the best detective."

She squeezes my arm. "I've always told Nathan you lack confidence but you're a bright girl." She winks. I feel sick.

"What are you two chatting about?" Suddenly Nathan is at our table. He has a fresh glass of champagne for his wife.

"Girl talk," Angela says without missing a beat.

"Great," Nathan says, taking his seat. He doesn't look at me.

Finally, the conversation is over, and I can breathe. But that relief is overtaken by another worry. There were red flags coming off Angela in waves. Does she know about me and Nathan? Is she our blackmailer?

15

We win the award. Angela kisses her husband on the mouth. Chet, Janine, and Vivian walk with us down to the stage, and Nathan thanks his wife and kids in our acceptance speech. Then he buys us all a round of drinks. I drink half a glass of champagne to join in. All the time, my hands are clammy and my eyes are drawn to Angela. She smiles with us. She takes group photos of us for the company website. She hugs Nathan and congratulates us all.

After the celebration, I consider when I can leave without seeming rude. Lucas Weathers has been a hovering addition this evening. While he's rarely at the table, he stops by and makes his presence known every so often. I decide to go to the bar for a while, even though I'm back to diet soda.

A few minutes after I sit down, Chet plops onto a bar stool next to me, his bourbon breath warm on my cheeks.

"Having fun?"

"A blast," I deadpan, staring at the alcohol-lined shelves of the bar.

My dry humor is lost on Chet. He's all but three sheets to

the wind by now. He tilts his head and slugs back the rest of the amber liquid in his glass and orders another, suppressing a belch. I give him a disgusted glance, but he doesn't take the hint and places a hand on my back.

I squirm away from him and lean so far to the left that I'm afraid I might slide right off the edge.

Chet's eyes roam across me like a hungry wolf. "You are hot as hell tonight."

"I think I liked the nice version of you better," I say. "The drunk you is annoying."

"Hey. I think you and I have a very nice back and forth. Don't you?"

I lift my glass to my lips again, saying nothing.

Chet's smile is sly, and his eyes glint with mischief. "Where'd you get it?"

"Get what?" I cut him an irritated scowl.

"The dress?"

"I don't remember," I lie, hoping to shut down the conversation.

"You are so boring sober. Why aren't you drinking, anyway? Preggo?"

"That is unbelievably rude." Then I soften. "I'm driving home tonight."

"You're not staying in the hotel? Why not? Everyone else is."

"Honestly, I just want to go home."

"You're still sore about that Davina Clothing thing." He points a finger in my direction. "You need to get over it. We've all been yelled at by a client. It's basically what we get paid for."

I disagree, but I don't argue with him.

"We all make mistakes," he continues. "The thing with

our industry is that as soon as you make a mistake, there's someone there to take advantage of it."

I turn to him sharply. "What do you mean?"

He pauses, staring at his fingers. "Well, like Vivian."

I nod. For a moment there, I thought he'd slipped up and admitted something important. I side-eye him, wondering.

Janine's laugh is like a fast-firing gun behind me. I spin on my barstool, intrigued to know what's going on at our table. She's gorgeous tonight. In the past, I might have been jealous of her skintight dress, but the events of the last few weeks have reminded me what is important and what isn't. What's important now is that Janine is drunk, and she has her hand on Nathan's arm. She leans into him, laughing at his jokes.

I see movement from the left—Angela returning from the bathroom. Nathan's wife stops, regarding Janine and Nathan in a clinch, and her cheeks turn a flaming-hot red.

Shit. After what I said about Janine and Nathan being close, this does not look good. Slipping down from the stool, I approach Janine and carefully clamp my hand around her wrist. I give it a firm tug away from Nathan, who also moves away from us both.

"What are you doing?" she slurs.

"Come with me," I say. "We'll get you some coffee."

"But I—"

Gently, I help her to her feet, hook her arm over my shoulder, and lead her away from the table. I dare not meet Angela's eye on our way to the bar.

"You can't do that," I whisper to her once we're out of earshot.

"Do what?" Janine leans against the bar, working hard to stay upright.

"You can't openly flirt with Nathan right in front of his wife."

"I... I wasn't."

"Yes, you were, hon," I say gently.

I order two coffees and carry them over to another table. Janine stumbles along behind me. Then I grab some bread from one of the baskets and hand it to her. She studies me, staring as if she underestimated me. Then her lips curl into a devious Cheshire cat smile.

"You're telling *me* not to flirt with the boss in front of his wife?"

"Yes." I swallow hard, not breaking her gaze. *Why the hell is she looking at me like she just won the lottery and I'm the first one she wants to brag to?*

Then I find out.

"Oh, honey." Janine hiccups.

Her eyes shutter a moment before another fit of laughter overtakes her. It's short-lived. Her face becomes stoic, and her smile vanishes. She clutches my shoulder and brings me closer.

Her voice is a sinister whisper, sending a chill through my spine. "I don't think *you* of all people should be the one giving me advice. After all, it was you I saw going into Nathan's hotel room that night at the retreat."

16

The drive home is a lonely one. I'm paranoid, checking for evidence of someone stalking me. Before I get in the car, I turn on my phone's flashlight and checked every single seat. I've seen horror movies where the killer slowly rises from the back seat. I'm *not* falling for that one.

Janine knows I slept with Nathan. Not only that, but she listened to me talk about meeting a guy in the bar and never once corrected me. Now it feels far too convenient for her to have gone to meet a friend instead of riding back with us in Nathan's car. Did she do it to give us an opportunity to talk or because she wanted to follow us and see what happened? Of course, we gave her everything she needed by screwing on that empty road. *Idiots.*

She was drunk tonight. I wonder if she'll even remember what she said to me. And if she is the blackmailer, why would she be so careless as to tell me what she saw? Unless it's part of the plan to keep me on edge. That seems to be the blackmailer's MO. The note to Nathan is a good example, a reminder that they aren't going away. It means soon they'll reveal their hand.

There's a loud horn blast behind me, and I shudder with shock. I check the mirror and notice a truck driving too close. *Am I driving slowly?* The speedometer suggests I'm barely under the speed limit. I press the gas slightly, pulling ahead of the truck. It speeds up. My heart feels like it's going to beat out of my chest. The road is busy, and this dick won't let up.

The first few spots of rain hit the windshield, and the wipers turn on with a screech. My fingers tighten against the steering wheel as the rain comes down harder. I've never been a confident night driver, and now bad weather and an irresponsible truck driver make it twice as hard. I suck in a deep breath, trying to calm my heart, then I ease off the gas a fraction, not wanting to go too fast in the rain.

The truck driver blasts his horn. I glance at my mirror again. Are they the blackmailer?

The rain thunders down. At the next junction, I pull off, my pulse throbbing strongly in my ears. When the truck zooms past, I let out a cry of surprise and relief. It was simply an impatient driver. For the rest of the drive home, I can relax and drive slowly. It will take longer, but I don't care.

About thirty minutes later, I park my Kia in the driveway and climb out. My legs are a little jellified from the adrenaline-filled drive. The rain comes down in sheets, and I grab my jacket, holding it over my head like a canopy. There's no sign of Mrs. Doebler tonight. Her lights aren't on. Even after midnight, she usually leaves a lamp on in her bedroom. I've always noticed that soft warm glow through the curtains.

But perhaps she's visiting her daughter. There's not much time to consider it when the rain rushes down. I hurry inside, lock the door, check that I've locked the door twice—it's my new routine—then hang up my jacket and run upstairs.

The tight red dress clings to my damp skin as I wriggle out of it. Shivering, I grab my robe and pull it on before removing my makeup and pulling out some PJs. Still wired from the drive, I head back to the kitchen to make a hot cup of cocoa. It's what my mom would do when I had bad dreams. A pang of grief hits me like a sharp, thin knife sliding between my ribs. I shrug it away.

While the milk heats up, I remember promising Vivian I'd call to let her know I was home. I think about texting instead, but I want to hear a woman's voice, perhaps because I'm remembering Mom. I grab my cell phone and find her in my contacts.

"Lucy," she says. "Are you home safe?"

"I'm fine. Thanks for checking in on me." I pause. There are road noises on the call. "Aren't you in the hotel?"

"We're heading out to a club," Vivian says. "It's all Chet's idea."

"Wow. Go you."

"I may live to regret this."

I hear voices in the background. Laughter, I think. "Is Janine okay?"

"She's in her hotel room," Vivian says. "She's fine—she's just wasted. But she sobered up a little, thanks to you."

"Okay. That's good."

"Listen, Luce, I've got to go, but I'll see you at work next week, okay?"

"Sure. Thanks, Viv."

The milk is boiling. I reduce the heat and stir in the hot chocolate powder. As always, I have every light on in my condo. The utility bills are going to be sky-high soon. Then my phone pings, and I turn sharply to view the new notification.

"Not again. Please not again," I say, my fingers reaching out for the phone.

When I see the notification, the spatula drops from my fingertips. I run to the front door, almost tripping over my shoes in the hallway. I snatch up my key from the bowl and jam it into the lock. By the time the door opens, there's no one there.

But on my phone, I saw a figure on my doorstep, clear as day, in the notification from my doorbell camera. Barefoot, I run down the drive to the road, checking left then right. I hear an engine, the unmistakable acceleration of someone wanting to get out of the area fast. I run into the middle of the empty street, squinting into the dark. There's the outline of a vehicle and two red lights in the distance. A large vehicle, I think, too far away for me to see the number plate. They must have really put their foot down to get away so fast. Unless the person at my door ran partway down the road to get into the car.

Or could it be a truck? My heart skips a beat. I back away from the road and hurry back to the condo. And it's there I freeze.

In my haste to get out of the condo and chase down the figure at the door, I hadn't noticed the package left on my doorstep. It's about the size of a cake box, wrapped in brown paper and tied together with twine. Slowly, I walk back toward the parcel. My breathing is unsteady. The cold air wisps through my lungs. I want to be in my home, and I want to feel safe, but this person has invaded my space, and my home will never feel safe again.

Before I pick up the parcel, I rush into the condo and

check the kitchen. I grab the package, hurry it over to the kitchen counter and leave it there, treating it like a bomb I don't want to touch. Then I lock the door and grab a knife. I dial the emergency services and wait.

What if someone slipped into the house? I can't bear it. This has to stop. I can't live like this any longer.

"Nine-One-One, what's your emergency?"

"Someone..." I pause. "There might be an intruder in my home."

"Which service do you require?" asks the calm female voice.

"Police."

17

The package sits on the counter in my kitchen. It looks innocuous, like a Christmas present ordered online. Yet I feel like at any moment, it could grow fangs and bite me. I shake my head, almost laughing at myself.

It's late. Adrenaline courses through me. My fingers twitch with impatience. *Where are the police?* As I pace the kitchen, my eyes linger on the parcel. *What is it?* A litany of terrible things flash through my mind—a bomb, poison, a dead animal, more photographs of me and Nathan. Something worse?

Then I check the window again, expecting someone out there staring in. A pale white face.

Sit down, Lucy. Calm the fuck down.

I take a seat at the table, get out my phone, and check through the events on my doorbell camera, finding the footage of the mystery person again. Then I save it to my phone just to be sure. The police will want to see this.

Zooming in doesn't yield any extra information. Whoever

it is has no identifiable features. A baseball cap obscures their eyes, and a mask hides the lower half of their face. They wear gloves, so there's no skin visible either. The hoodie and sweats are baggy enough to hide their body shape. The one thing I do notice is that they seem like either a fairly short man or a tall woman—I would estimate their height to be about five foot nine. Pretty average. Basically, there's nothing to go on at all. I chastise myself for not getting a better view of the vehicle. If only I'd managed to see the plates.

A few minutes later, the police cruiser rolls into my driveway—discreet, no siren, no flashing lights. This is a relief. Two officers approach my door, one male, one female. I open the door before they've even ascended my front porch steps, waving them inside.

"Evening, ma'am," the male officer, whose badge reads Officer Briggs, says. "We received an emergency call to this address. There was an intruder in your home? Are they still here?" The porch light picks out the brown flecks of his eyes. His fingertips hover near the gun strapped to his hip.

"That was me." I nod, trying to keep my hands from shaking too visibly. I show them into the hall and take them through to my small kitchen. "It wasn't an intruder exactly. Someone left a package. I know that doesn't sound... bad. But if you could see the doorbell footage, it's clear it's meant to be a threat of some sort."

"Is that it?" The woman—Officer Calypso, according to her name badge—points at the offending box sitting on my counter. Her chestnut hair is pulled into a tight no-nonsense ponytail. She's much shorter than her partner but carries herself with confidence.

"Yes," I reply. "I picked it up and brought it in here, but I haven't opened it yet. I was scared to."

Officer Briggs brushes gloved fingers across the edges of the box, inspecting its corners. He lifts his head and regards me. "How long ago did the package come?"

I check the microwave clock. "About thirty minutes ago."

"And you said it was on your front porch?" Officer Calypso asks, her jaw working as she chews gum.

"Yes. I got a notification from my doorbell camera. As you can imagine, that was a bit scary, given that it's so late. I saw the person from the camera. Then I went out there to see what was going on. I ran down to the road, and a truck, or something large, pulled out and sped off, but I didn't get their plates."

The two officers exchange an unreadable glance. Officer Calypso steps closer, her eyes roaming over the box. "There was no name or anything on it?"

I shake my head.

"Can we see the video footage?" Officer Briggs asks.

"Sure." I load the app and push the screen in their direction. "You can see that whoever it is has a mask on. I wasn't able to tell their gender."

Officer Calypso's eyes narrow on the footage. She chews her gum. I wonder if it's a nervous habit. It's certainly making *me* nervous.

"Have you received any other suspicious packages or mail?" Calypso asks, reverting her eyes to me.

I sit down in my chair, exhausted. With my eyes fixed on my fingers, I nod. I have to tell them. The police can't do their job unless I do. And yes, I understand the consequences, especially to Nathan's marriage. But it's too late now. I can't stop this from happening.

"I'm being blackmailed." A hand flies up to my mouth. I'm shocked I said the words out loud. "About four weeks ago, I went on a work retreat and I... I slept with my boss. My married boss. Someone found out. They... took a photo. Now they're threatening me and my boss. They want money."

During the next fifteen minutes, I show Calypso and Briggs the text messages on my phone, including the horribly embarrassing photo of me and Nathan together. When I start to cry out of sheer humiliation, Calypso gets up and pours me a cup of coffee. Then she pours one for herself.

"I wouldn't usually," she says. "Not at this time. But this is a lot to take in."

Briggs refuses a cup. He sighs deeply, his eyes meeting mine. I feel like he's trying to size me up and figure out whether I'm crazy or scared. He scratches the part in his jet-black hair and smiles at his partner when she takes a seat.

I sip the coffee. "Please don't tell Nathan's wife. She doesn't deserve this. We made a stupid mistake, and we're so sorry for it."

"We'll try to keep the details of the case under wraps until we have more evidence," Calypso says.

"Thank you." I blow out a breath of relief through parted lips.

"Now," Briggs says. "What is your security like in this condo? Do you have cameras at the back?"

"No," I admit. "There's a yard, but I don't have any cameras."

"It might give you some peace of mind. Someone came onto your property. That's a red flag right there. If you like, I'll take a quick look around. I know you were worried about leaving the door open while you investigated outside."

"Thank you so much." I'm pleasantly surprised by how understanding these cops are being.

"As for the package," Briggs continues. "It's not ticking. I doubt it's anything dangerous. But we'll take it to the station, get forensics on it." He stands. "I'll do my sweep while Calypso here takes an official statement. That sound good?"

I nod, honestly relieved that he's walking me through this process so well. He nods back to me and leaves the kitchen while Calypso opens up her pad and clicks her pen. Together, we work through a timeline of events, culminating in tonight. She marks everything down in between sips of coffee.

"All done, and all clear." Briggs returns, smiling. "I checked that your windows are locked too. So you can sleep well tonight knowing you're safe. Okay? But if you have any more issues, call us again."

"That's right." Calypso pours her coffee into the sink and grabs the box from the counter. "I'm sure this is nothing but an empty threat, but we'll get the professionals to open this at the precinct. You get some rest now. Remember what Briggs said. He isn't pretty, but he's usually right." She grins.

I smile because Briggs is handsome, with his flecked eyes and umber skin. "Thank you," I say, leading them to the door, my bones rattling and my stomach turning upside down.

Officer Calypso halts on my porch and swivels her tiny body toward me, smacking her gum. "Stay safe, now, Lucy. Keep us in the loop, especially if you hear from the blackmailer again. I don't want you making any rash decisions."

"I'll keep that in mind. Thank you."

I watch them exit my driveway in their patrol car, wondering if I've turned a corner in this nightmare or made things worse. I guess I'll have to wait to find out.

I check my doors and windows twice before I allow myself to get in bed. I keep the lights on and the covers tucked around my chin and lie there like a picture of a person frozen in time. A still life—that's me. I'm a prisoner. Wherever I go and whatever I do, there's someone walking with me, shadowing me. But who?

18

I'm surprised and relieved when Nathan answers his phone the next morning. Part of me had wondered if he was done with me altogether. As I tell him about the mysterious parcel hand delivered to my condo, I hear his kids playing in the background.

"Did you open it?" he asks.

"No. I was too scared."

"Okay. Well, I have to drop Madeleine at a swimming lesson, but I could come to yours and take a look at it if you're concerned."

I close my eyes and let out a long sigh. "No, Nathan. I called the police, and they took it away. I told them everything, Nathan. All of it. You and me. Everything."

Nathan is silent on the other end, but I can almost feel him seething. A moment later, I hear footsteps. The sound of children playing is gone.

"What did you do, Lucy? Why?"

"Someone came to my home and left a threat. You're

fucked in the head if you think I'm not calling the police about that."

"Well, now you've fucked me," he snaps. "My marriage is over."

"Honestly, that's the least of my worries. I'm trying to stay alive here, Nathan. People are turning up at my home with suspicious packages."

"Remember, Lucy, they can't get money out of a dead person."

"Yeah? Well, how do we even know this is about the money? It's not like they've given us a drop-off point or any terms."

"I know. I'm sorry." He pauses. "God, what a mess. I'm sorry it's come to this."

"Me too," I admit. "For what it's worth, the police told me they'd be discreet. And I believed them. They were decent. They even checked the condo to make sure no one slipped in while I was trying to figure out who left the parcel."

"What do you mean?"

"I went outside to see if I could see them get away."

"On your own? Lucy, please be careful."

I want to point out that he didn't seem so bothered about my welfare before, but I keep quiet.

"I need to go," he says. "Call me if you find anything out about the box. Did you give the police my number?"

"Yes."

"Okay, well, I guess I'll wait for their call." He sounds a little deflated.

I don't feel too sorry for him when I hang up the call. After all, he's been flippant about my welfare this whole time and tried to make me feel guilty about calling the police. I won't forget Nathan's selfish streak for a long time. Him separating from his wife would be better in the long run. She deserves better.

It's still early. I'm hungry, tired, and shaken. But I grab my keys and head out the door. It's time to buy a security camera —a *real* security camera, not the cheap doorbell kind. That way, I can set it up in the yard. Maybe I'll invest in some extra locks on my doors. I may no longer feel safe in my own home, but I refuse to be a prisoner in it.

I'm on the floor of my living room, reading the one-hundred-twenty-page installation guide for the security camera, when my phone rings. My heart jumps into my throat. It's the police department.

"Lucy Croft?"

"Yes?"

"This is Officer Calypso. We met last night when we got a call out to your house about a suspicious package."

"That's me," I croak. I sit down and stuff an unruly strand of hair behind my ear.

"We successfully opened the package to investigate the contents inside," she says, her professional voice coming through like a gentle breeze through my phone.

"And...?" I can't breathe until she tells me what it was.

"Our evidence team discovered a bracelet inside."

"A bracelet?" I frown, feeling a mixture of disappointment and relief ripple through me. "That's it?"

"Yes, ma'am. We were wondering if you had time to stop by the station to identify it. See if you recognize it or if it has any significant meaning to you."

I stand up, tuck the phone in between my shoulder and

ear, cross my arms, and pace my living room. The boxes and instructions from the security camera and all the extra locks are sprawled out all over the floor, so I have to maneuver around them, kicking them out of the way.

"Yeah, uh, of course. Absolutely. I can do that. Today?"

"Whenever you're ready," Officer Calypso says.

I glance around for my keys and purse, momentarily forgetting where I tossed them after I got home from the hardware store. I locate them underneath one of the new key boxes and bend to pick them up with a grunt.

"I'll come now," I say.

My pulse quickens until it whooshes through my ears. This makes very little sense to me. I don't even recall losing a bracelet recently, and I can't remember wearing a bracelet at the work retreat. The most logical answer is that the black-mailer went into Nathan's room or car, found a bracelet, and assumed it was mine.

Perhaps it's really Nathan's wife's bracelet, or I forgot I was wearing one when we had sex. Either way, I'm on edge as I get back into my car and drive down to the station. My arms are cold. I left in such a hurry I didn't throw on a jacket.

Briggs greets me at reception and takes me to an interview room. It's my first time inside a room like this. My arms turn to gooseflesh. But he's all smiles and pleasantries, clearly attempting to put me at ease.

"I could get you a coffee from the machine, but it honestly tastes like piss," he says.

"I'm good. But thanks."

"Right, well, here we are." He pushes a teal box across the table. A jewelry box.

I peer closer, examining the silver bracelet inside. It makes sense now. The bracelet isn't from the work retreat.

It's what I wore to the awards ceremony. I instinctively touch my wrist. I didn't even notice it was gone when I arrived home.

"Do you recognize this bracelet?" Briggs asks.

I blink and scratch my cheek. "Yeah——" I clear my throat and readjust myself in my seat. "Yes. It's my bracelet. But I don't understand. I wore it last night. How... how did they do all this last night?"

"What do you mean?" Briggs asks.

"The box. The string. I don't get it."

He frowns. "It sounds premeditated. Whoever sent this to you had the box ready in their vehicle. They stole the bracelet, wrapped it, and drove it to you." He scratches a smattering of dark stubble across his jawline. "It takes me a long time to wrap a present—I'm not gonna lie. But maybe this person is good at it."

I nod. The fact that so much thought went into this makes me feel sick.

"Whoever sent this wanted to scare you. And they wanted to get close to you. I don't like that," Briggs says. "Now, we've got forensics working on the box. But help me out here. Who got close to you last night?"

I intertwine my fingers as I reel off a list of the people I sat with last night. As I speak, I think about each of them carefully because they are all suspects now.

Angela. I sat with her for a long time. We even embraced.

Janine. She was wasted. But could it have been an act to throw me off the scent?

Chet. He sat at the bar and flirted with me. Perhaps he used that as a distraction to steal the bracelet.

Vivian. We were close briefly—long enough for her to do this?

At least I can cross Nathan off the list. I purposefully stayed as far away from him as I could.

"You were sitting next to your boss's wife after the two of you had an affair?" Briggs asks. He lifts his eyebrows.

My cheeks flush with heat. "She told me that she thinks Nathan is... well, having an affair."

"Interesting. Well, Ms. Croft, I'm sorry, but I don't think there's going to be much chance of us keeping this information from Nathan Robertson's wife. She had the opportunity to steal that bracelet."

"But how would she deliver it? She was drinking, so she couldn't drive. And she was with Nathan. He would've mentioned if she left for at least an hour."

"Let us piece this puzzle together, Ms. Croft," he says. "You concentrate on staying safe. But you might want to give your boss a heads-up. We need to speak to him and his wife about this."

19

It takes me all of Saturday and Sunday to fit the new cameras and work out the apps that go with them. By Monday morning, I'm groggy with a hangover. These days, I need to drink red wine to help me sleep. It's the only thing that works.

"Are you all right?" Nathan asks. For once, he seems genuinely concerned.

"Do I look that bad?" I don't need him to answer that—I already know I look terrible.

He shakes his head, but his eyes have trouble meeting mine. I can see he feels guilty about all this. We're in the conference room. He's paranoid about us being alone in his office together, and to be honest, I get it. I don't want to do anything extra that could potentially raise questions about us, especially since I'm still suspicious about everyone in this office anyway.

The shades are drawn, but Nathan is still handsome under the subdued lighting. His arm rests on the surface of the table, his fingers laced together. His expression remains somewhat pained.

"Did you give your statement to the police?" I ask.

He nods. "This morning. Over the phone."

I sigh. I can tell from Nathan's demeanor that Briggs and Calypso haven't contacted Angela yet. It's only a matter of time before they do, and now I need to break the bad news. "I'm sorry about all this, Nathan."

His eyes reach mine. "You don't have anything to be sorry about, Lucy."

I see someone walk by the door, so I pretend to be inspecting a document that I've brought in here. The papers are just for show, to make it appear as though we're working on something. We don't know where to go to talk alone. It seems like nowhere is private anymore. Not even my own house.

"I have some bad news to break to you," I say. "The police... they're going to want to speak to Angela. Someone stole the bracelet from my wrist and delivered it back to me in a gift box."

"What?"

"Yeah. It's messed up. But the thing is... I sat next to Angela all night and—"

"It wasn't her," he snaps.

I lift a palm to calm him. "I'm not saying she did it. I'm saying that she's a suspect because of us sitting together."

He rakes his fingers through his hair. "So this is it. This is the end of my marriage."

"I'm sorry."

"Stop saying that," he chides.

"Okay, I will. To be honest, Nathan, she knows anyway. She spent the whole night talking about you and whether you're having an affair. She even asked me to be her eyes and ears in the office. It was awful. I didn't know what to say."

"She did?" His eyes widen. "God. I had no idea."

"Then Janine got drunk and flirted with you, which didn't help matters."

"So she thinks I'm screwing Janine?" He laughs. "You can't make this up."

"I wish we'd made this up." I rub my upper arms, thinking about the doorbell video. I showed it to Nathan this morning. It has been a wakeup call for me.

He places a tentative hand on my arm. "Lucy, I should have taken this more seriously. I'm sorry if I've been a bit… aloof. I've been so paranoid and feeling like I need to keep my family together. I kept thinking some hacker had our lines tapped or something. Or my office." I watch his eyes scan me as if he hopes I'll absorb every word he says and forgive him. But I can't say it. I don't feel it or even trust him.

"So the police have this number?" Nathan asks.

"Yeah, but it's a burner phone." I glance at the door leading out to the office. "It's one of them. I can feel it. If the police don't figure it out, we might end up continuing to work with the person stalking and blackmailing us. How are we going to do that?" I sigh. "This is it now. I'm going to have to quit. Your marriage is going to end, and I'm going to lose my job. That's where we are now. I don't think this person even cares about the money. They just want us gone."

"The motive isn't money—it's our jobs?" Nathan's eyes follow mine to outside the room. "Chet. It has to be. I'll kill him—"

When Nathan moves to get up, I grab his arm and pull him down. "We don't know that. We have to let the police handle this. Promise me you won't do anything stupid. We have to carry on as normal. One wrong move, and they'll figure it out and... I don't know. Either escalate or get out of here, I guess."

"You're right. But I hate this."

I smile, not because I'm happy about this nightmare but because finally, Nathan is on the same page as me. He leans back in his chair, tracing his jawline with his fingers. He does this sometimes when he's thinking hard about something.

Before all this happened, these were the subtle mannerisms that attracted me. I'd wanted to know him, smell him, feel his touch. He's still handsome, but I no longer crave him in that primal, physical way. Now he represents the fear of this hell. When I gaze into his eyes, I see my own weaknesses reflected back.

"I've gone over and over what to do," I say. "Before I called the police, I mean."

Nathan's eyes roam over my face as if he wants to tap into my thoughts and emotions straight from the source. "Like what? I'm open to hearing it."

I shrug. "I was ready to find the money, to be honest. But now that the police are involved, do you really think it's a good idea to pay this person?"

Nathan sighs and leans back in his chair. He rocks back and forth. The chair makes a squeaking noise that sets me on edge.

After a moment of contemplation, he pushes away from the table and stands up. "I need to get back to work, but we will think this over, all right?"

I nod, disappointment crumbling inside me.

Nathan must notice because he pauses before walking to the door. "Hey, Lucy?"

"Hmm?" I glance up at him.

"Everything is going to work out. I'm on your side. I'll help you through this. If you are ever scared, day or night, call me. Give me every detail of what's happening, and we'll take it to the police together. All right?"

I inhale slowly. "All right."

I want to believe in his promises, but I'm afraid to trust him. I can't trust anyone. Maybe not even the police.

When I'm in the office now, I forever count down the clock until the end of the day. My skin crawls every time someone walks over to my desk. Chet brings me coffee in the afternoon and tries to chat with me about a client. Vivian wants advice about the Davina contract. And all through the day, I'm sweating, aching to be away from those people.

Because I'm in such a hurry to get away, I stumble straight into another person on my trek through the parking lot to my car after work one day. "Sorry," I say, frazzled, as I brush my windswept hair out of my face and glance up to see who I almost knocked over.

My stomach takes a roller-coaster dive. Angela stands there, stunning and tall in her slimming black leggings and black tank top. She could be on her way to model for an athletic-wear clothing line.

"Angela." I can't hide the surprise in my voice. "Sorry, you startled me."

"I didn't mean to. Are you okay, Lucy? You seemed distracted, like you were searching for someone."

"Oh, no." I swat a dismissive hand, but it feels like an entire colony of bees has been let loose underneath my skin.

"I try to be aware in the parking lot after work, you know? Just to make sure I'm safe."

"I totally get it." She moves back toward her car when the little boy in the car seat beats his fists against the plastic frame. "Sorry, got to get this terror out. Won't be a minute."

"Oh, that's okay. I've got to get going."

She seems deflated. "Please stay. Just for a moment." She breathes heavier, her cheeks pink as she tries to lift a squirming five-year-old from his car seat. He bucks his hips, flailing arms and legs that get caught in the harness straps.

"Move your leg, sweetie," she says, attempting to maneuver a tiny kicking foot.

Next, he throws his juice box container at her and wails.

Angela brushes her hair away from her face, rolls her eyes, and groans. "Sorry. They didn't have a nap today, so it's tantrum city right now."

"Oh, it's fine. Do you need help with anything?"

She may not be aware of it, but watching her like this... the guilt eats me alive. Like I'm being dipped into a vat of acid one body part at a time. Angela grabs her purse from the back of the car and slams the door. Her two unruly kids swing off both her arms.

"Mommy, can I have a snack?" asks a little girl in pigtails. She whines for Angela's phone, making grabby hands to snatch it from her mother. Angela lets go of the boy, who then tries to climb the hood of the car.

"Don't do that," Angela groans as if she has one fiber of patience left and it's about to snap in half.

"You've really got your hands full." I offer a sympathetic smile.

Angela rolls her eyes. "That's the understatement of the year. Anyway, I wanted to apologize for oversharing with you

that night of the awards ceremony." She yanks her boy from
the hood of the car by the back of his shirt. He screeches, but
he laughs.

"I don't think you were oversharing. We were just chatting," I reassure her.

Angela's face relaxes a little. "Well, thank you for lending
a listening ear."

"Anytime. I hope things are going better for you." I make
this comment to feel her out and see what she's thinking
about now that she's sober. Maybe since she's frazzled, her
guard will be lowered.

Angela stands closer to me with barely an inch between
us. She whispers as if she doesn't want anyone overhearing
what she says next. "I still think Nathan is cheating on me."
The vindictiveness in her voice makes my blood turn to ice.
"And I'm trying to find evidence to prove it."

"I'm sorry to hear that."

Her smile returns, her face glowing. It's like she switched
to another personality entirely. "Can I ask you something—if
you promise to keep it between us?"

*What could she possibly want to share that doesn't involve
someone getting hurt?*

"Sure."

"Have you noticed anything going on between Nathan
and Janine?"

"Janine?"

"Yes, Janine. Young, pretty Janine, who got drunk and
flirted with my husband the other night." Her eyes are wild,
and I want to back away. She has one hand wrapped around
her son's wrist. The other is idly playing with her daughter's
pigtail.

"I... I don't think so." I sense that this is a trap, and I need to swim to safety. I glance at my phone, pretending to receive a call. "I'm sorry, this is my dad. He had a medical procedure done today. I'd better get this." I pretend to push the answer button and press the phone to my ear. "Have a good evening, Angela." I wave to her as I scurry away in the direction of my car.

Angela continues to regard me. Her kids squirm out of her grip and race each other in circles around their car. She doesn't pay any attention to them—she stares right at me instead.

I wait until I'm in my car to pull the phone from my ear and clutch the steering wheel until my knuckles turn white. I take a shaky breath, start the engine, and drive away from this awkward situation and Angela's skeptical stare.

20

I spot Nathan sitting on a pine-green park bench. He's wearing a black T-shirt that hugs his broad chest, watching the playground, smiling. As I walk closer. Children's squealing drowns out the street noise. Nathan turns his head toward me, and the smile fades. But he nods a hello.

"Hey," I say, sitting next to him. "You called me. What's up?"

I notice Nathan's son on the climbing frame, dangling by one arm. His tongue pokes out as he concentrates and swings to the next loop. He's as boisterous as he was in the parking lot yesterday.

Nathan pulls his attention away from his son and sighs. "I got another threatening letter."

"Do you have it?"

"I have it." His jaw flexes.

My eyes roam the length of the playground, but there's no one around us except children. Nathan's kid jumps down from the climbing frame and heads over to the sandbox. He huddles down with a little boy shoveling sand into a bucket.

"That's your boy, isn't it?" I ask, nodding in his direction. "I bumped into Angela getting them out of the car yesterday. That was awkward."

Nathan stretches his legs out in front of him. "Yeah, Carson. Madeline is with Angela. She has dance class."

"Oh."

Nathan slips his hand into his pocket and unfolds a yellow piece of paper that could have been torn from a legal pad. It's folded into quarters. He inconspicuously slides it into my open palm. I glance around, making sure no one is watching.

"You probably should've put this in a plastic bag or something," I say, slowly unfolding it. "If I take this to the police, it'll have our fingerprints on it."

He shrugs. "I didn't think. Sorry."

You went to the police. I don't like that at all. Keep working with them, and things will only get worse. It's time to pay up, Nathan. Time is running out. Ticktock. Twenty thousand. You know the number.

Despite the fact that I knew what kind of note it would be, my heart pounds against my ribs. I tell my body to stop reacting. I need a clear head. Lifting the sheet, I examine it more closely. The letters have been written with a ballpoint pen. I wonder if the person allowed their hand to drag along the page, leaving traces of DNA. There's a chance they wore gloves. If it were me, I'd wear gloves.

"We should take this to the police. There's so much they can analyze here. The pen brand, the handwriting, fingerprints—"

"It says not to go to the cops."

I stare at him incredulously. "Of course, it's going to say that. But we need the cops. They're our only protection."

He turns to me. "It says things are going to get worse. I don't like that. I think we should pay."

"Look at me, Daddy!"

Carson is on the swings now, and Nathan waves to him. He's in a gray T-shirt with a T. rex picture and wears navy blue shorts. His tiny fists clutch the chains as he throws his head back in a cackling laugh, pumping his legs with the swing's momentum. He seems happier, more carefree than he did in the parking lot with Angela the other day.

"Do you recognize the handwriting?" Nathan asks.

"No, do you?"

He shakes his head. "It looks like whoever wrote it is trying to keep their handwriting unidentifiable."

I stare at a tree branch moving in the breeze. "I don't think we should do anything until we take this to the police."

Nathan's eyes are bloodshot and hopeless as he returns my gaze. "I don't know what to do."

I shift my weight, my hands still buried deep in my pockets. "Have the cops contacted Angela yet? They sounded like they would."

"No. Unless she hasn't told me, but that seems unlikely." He lets out a humorless bark of a laugh. "Maybe they've dropped it. There are killers on the street, and we've got some idiot sending us handwritten notes and dropping off a bracelet at your house."

"I know, it's weird," I say.

"They haven't harmed us, have they? Maybe they're not going to. Maybe we can make all of this go away, and you can tell the police to drop it."

"How would we even pay? We don't have the money."

"True."

"Let me take it to the police." I lift the note to indicate what I mean.

Nathan is quiet. His hands are clasped in his lap. He stares at them. He seems defeated today, and I'm surprised by his switch in demeanor. I'm getting a crash course in Nathan's coping mechanisms. He either goes into denial or becomes deflated.

"Nathan, please don't get upset by what I'm about to say, but we need to explore all options," I begin softly.

His eyebrows knit, and he lifts his head to meet my gaze. "Okay..."

I lick my lips, choosing my words carefully. "Are you *sure* your wife isn't the one behind all this?"

Nathan is already shaking his head before I get the whole sentence out. "It's not Angela. She can't be involved."

She already suspects you're cheating on her, I think, but I don't say it aloud. He already seems like he's one frayed wire away from combusting as it is.

"Any other people you think it could be?" I ask.

Nathan's upper lip twitches, and he studies a cracker on the ground by his feet. Ants have started accumulating there, busily trying to pick it apart. "We should circle back around to our first plan."

"What plan?"

Nathan's eyes remain fixed on the cracker and the ants. "The plan to come up with the money."

I exhale a long breath and pause, not wanting to immediately protest. "Nathan, we need to let the police handle—"

"I have an idea. Will you at least hear me out?"

"Yes," I say, frustrated.

"I think I might be able to get some money from the company, but only about five grand."

I stare at him, stunned. "From the company? What, like an advance on your wages?"

"No. Like, we take it from the company."

"What? You mean, like fraud?"

Nathan frowns. "I prefer the term *loan*, but yes, essentially."

I drop my head into my hands.

"Don't dismiss it outright," he says. "We could end this, and quickly, if we pay them off."

I lift my head. "No. Absolutely not. We aren't criminals."

"No, but our lives may depend on this. We're being backed into a corner. I can feel it."

"You're being dramatic. Even if we are capable of getting the money, who's to say that after they get paid, they'll leave us alone? What if they want more or find other ways to threaten us?"

Nathan's face pales as if he's going to pass out or be sick. "We don't know that, Lucy. We just have to hope for the best."

"But even if you 'borrowed'"—I use air quotes because I know he wouldn't pay the company back—"the five thousand, how do we come up with the other fifteen..." I drift off, watching Nathan. He's on his feet, his face fixed on the playground. "What is it?"

"Carson isn't on the swings anymore."

I stand. "Try the climbing frame."

"Carson?"

Shielding my eyes from the sun, I search the area for a T. rex shirt. Some of the moms stare our way, sensing trouble. Nathan jogs over to the swings, and I follow. His little boy is gone.

21

It's amazing how quickly the air in the playground stills. Children run to their parents. They aren't squealing with joy anymore. They're quiet. Nathan is the one darting across the playground, screaming Carson's name. I call out for Carson, too, though I wonder if he'd even come to me. He doesn't know me.

A few of the parents join in, counting their own kids to make sure he isn't mixed in with a group, checking inside the climbing frame, and shouting his name. When it's clear he isn't in the play area, we venture farther afield, making our way across the green stretch of park beyond. My heart is pounding.

The playground isn't that large, and I don't see many places for kids to hide. I don't know Nathan's children well, so I can't say if Carson would be the type to run away, but even if he did, why now? He was on the swing, pumping his little legs, giggling as he soared into the sky. My stomach clenches. I see the wild terror in Nathan's eyes, and my chest feels tight.

"What does your little boy look like?" A pretty woman

with thin dreadlocks framing her face directs the question to me, and I almost flounder.

Now isn't the time to correct someone. "He's wearing a gray T-shirt with a T. rex on the front. Blue shorts. Light-brown hair."

"Got it." She wanders over to a group of moms to relay the information.

Nathan jogs over to me. "Have they seen him?"

"No, but everyone in the park is searching for him. It's going to be okay, Nathan. We'll find him." But even as I say the words, my palms sweat. I can't be sure of that. Not after the last few weeks.

"I need to call the police." Nathan runs a hand through his hair. "How long has it been?"

"Five minutes," I say. "I'll call them if you like."

My phone is halfway out of my pocket when there's a shout and a commotion over by a cluster of trees. "He's over here!"

Nathan is off, sprinting across the grass. I follow behind, jogging more slowly, relieved to see a woman with shoulder-length wavy blond hair holding hands with a boy in a T. rex shirt.

They aren't far away, maybe fifty feet at the most. Once Nathan reaches them, the woman lets go of his hand, taps Nathan on the back, and smiles. I catch up with them, a little out of breath. Carson is crying quietly, probably shaken by all the commotion, and Nathan pulls him into a big bear hug. That tight ache in my stomach finally uncoils.

"Thank *God* you're okay." Nathan straightens up and musses Carson's hair. "You had us worried for a minute there, kiddo."

"Sorry, Daddy," he says.

"It's okay, buddy, I'm not angry. I was just scared is all. Why did you run off like that?"

Carson rubs his fingers across his eyes and stares at me before he answers Nathan. "I didn't run off, Daddy."

I sense that he's shy with a new person around, so I take a step back. But as I do, my eyes are drawn to Carson's fingers. One hand is clenched into a tiny fist.

"What do you mean you didn't run off? How did you get over here?" Nathan crouches down to speak to his son.

"Nathan," I say softly. "Look at his hand. It's like he's holding something."

Nathan frowns, his eyes journeying southward. "What do you have, bud?" He pries Carson's fingers open and lifts a piece of paper from Carson's palm.

No, no, no, no, no. Not Nathan's kid, too. I close my eyes to stem the wave of dizziness that washes over me. Writing threatening text messages, sabotaging my work, sending blackmail letters, and turning up to my condo are all one thing. But a child? It's sick. We're stuck in this sick game.

When I open my eyes again, Nathan is unfolding the paper, which looks to be the same size as a regular letter. He glances at it then clutches it to his chest, hiding the contents.

"What is it?" I ask. "Show me."

I'm concerned he might throw up, he's so pale. *How bad can it be? Another threat?* At least Carson won't understand what it means. Even if he can read already, he wouldn't get the nuances of the threat.

Nathan thrusts the page toward me, and I back away, instinctively protecting Carson from what might be written there. My stomach drops. There is no note. It's a photograph. It's *the* photograph of me and Nathan having sex in his car.

I fold it and put it in my pocket, no longer caring about

forensics or anything like that. Then I rest my back against a tree, catching my breath.

"He won't be able to tell what it is," I say, my voice raw with emotion. "It's too blurry."

"That bastard," Nathan says between his teeth.

"Daddy swore."

I'm relieved to see that Carson is cheering up a little. I try to rearrange my face into a smile.

"Where did you get this, Carson?" Nathan asks, keeping his voice soft. Only I hear the tremble.

The boy's eyes skate to me, and the coy expression returns to his face. He flicks his gaze to the ground as if he doesn't want to answer that question in front of me.

Nathan picks up on this, glancing up at me, then back down at his son. He stands up, brushing the dirt from his knees. He walks over to me. "Can I have it?"

I pass him the picture, and Nathan stomps to the trash can, tearing the paper into bits along the way. His eyes meet with mine briefly, but I have to turn away.

Nathan grabs Carson's hand and coaxes him toward the parking lot. "Come on, Carson. It's time to go home." On his way past me, Nathan meets my gaze. "This has to end."

I nod, unable to use words right now. My body is frozen in fear.

22

Some creep cornered Nathan's five-year-old son at the playground and handed him a picture of his father having sex with another woman. It's sickening. I can hardly stand it. I'm shaking all the way home. When I walk into my condo, I check that every door and window is locked, swipe through the security-camera apps, and then open a bottle of vodka and slosh two fingers into a tumbler. My throat is still burning from the liquor when Nathan calls.

"How's Carson?" I ask.

Nathan lets out a long breath. "I had to buy him an ice cream and let him pick out a toy to stop him telling his mother. Though at this point, I'm not sure it's even worth keeping it from her anymore."

"You need to tell her this. Your child came face-to-face with our stalker. *Her* child. This is beyond me and you now. She needs to understand that her kids are in danger."

On the other end of the line, I can hear Nathan weeping. "I fucked up so bad."

Anger spreads through me like the vodka from ten

minutes ago. "Pull yourself together right now. This isn't helping anyone. Get your act together, Nathan, because I'm sick of this. We've been in this together from day one, but you've made stupid mistake after stupid mistake."

He sniffs loudly. "I know. Sorry."

"Did Carson give you a description of the blackmailer? We need that more than anything."

"He said it was a man. But he didn't describe Chet. So either it isn't someone from the office, or one of them has hired a lacky."

I nod. "I think there's two people working here. I thought that when the bracelet turned up at my condo."

"So, how much can you get? We need twenty. I can raise ten. What about you?"

"Are you serious? You're not taking this to the police?"

"You mean the police who haven't followed up on our statements? The ones that have done jack shit? This is my child, Lucy—my fucking child—and I need it to be sorted. Now. I can raise ten grand. Five of my own, five from the company. What can you bring to the table?"

I tell him my last resort. The one card up my sleeve that I hoped I wouldn't have to use. "My dad will lend me the money. I can get ten grand."

"Good." He hangs up.

I sit on the edge of my bed, staring at the number on my phone screen. I know what I have to do. It's just a matter of hitting the call button and following through with it. I take a deep breath and rub my clammy palms on my thighs.

"Come on, Lucy. You can do this."

I try to give myself a mental pep talk. I remind myself that this is my last resort and I have no choice. Nathan was right about this blackmailer and about the police. If we can get the money, maybe we can make all of this go away.

I've already made a decision about what to do once the money goes to this horrible person—I'm quitting. I'm going home to live with Dad. Let's face it—I haven't been right since Mom died, and I need to start over once I put all of this behind me.

I hit the call button, wait a beat, then the line starts ringing. Before I have a chance to bow out, the familiar comforting voice of my father cheerily says, "Hello? Is that my baby girl calling me?"

Instant guilt and sorrow, regret and embarrassment flood my consciousness. "Hey, Dad."

"Sweetie?" My father's voice is laced with concern. "What's going on? Is everything okay?"

Do it. Tell him. You don't have to give him details, but the quicker you rip off the Band-Aid, the quicker the anxiety will subside.

"Well," I begin with some nervous laughter. "I actually called to talk to you about something important. A problem I'm having."

There's a pause. "Sure, Lucy. You know I'm always here to lend a listening ear."

"Thanks. Unfortunately, this time, I might need you to lend more than just a listening ear." It's a perfect setup. I can't waste the opportunity. If I wimp out now, I'll never get it said. I picture Nathan's son with the printed picture in his hand. I keep thinking about how this will end once I do what I need to do.

"Okay..." My father waits for me to elaborate.

"Dad, I need to borrow some money. I'm having a bit of a situation. I can't really talk about it right now or give you a reason, but I'm in some trouble, and I need it. I'm really sorry to have to tell you this over the phone and to spring this on you on such short notice." I'm barely able to choke the words out because I'm crying now.

"Okay, sweetie, calm down. We'll get this sorted."

My dad's kind voice, his tender heart. I blow out a breath, and the weight of the world comes out with it. "Thank you, Dad."

"Oh, Lucy. I'm so worried now. But we'll sort it out together, I promise. Dry your tears, honey."

"Okay." I sniffle and wipe my nose with a tissue. "I'll pay you back. I promise."

"Well, you'll have to. I know where you live, remember?" He chuckles.

"I mean it, Dad. This is all my fault. I swear I'll make it up to you."

"There's nothing to make up. You're a good girl, Lucy, and you always have been. Whatever this is, I still know you have a good heart."

"Dad, don't. I'll cry again."

"It's true. Your mom and I always knew that. Now, go and have a stiff drink. We'll talk tomorrow because the banks are closed now anyway."

After we both hang up, I collapse onto my bed and allow the tension in my neck and shoulders to release. For the first time since this started, I begin to think this might be it, the end of this nightmare.

23

Nathan chose a café outside of town for meeting up with me. It was about a thirty-minute drive, but I didn't really mind. In the grand scheme of things, it is probably safer this way. The less prying eyes on us, the better.

Still, I can't shake the sensation that we are still being followed everywhere we go, even if I never see anyone blatantly suspicious. This blackmailer has no rules. They aren't afraid to cross boundaries. It's like they want to mess with us as much as they want the money. I feel like no matter what we do or how far away we drive, the blackmailer will always remain one step ahead of us. Neither Nathan, nor I, has talked to the police about the latest incident at the playground. As Nathan said, it's time to stop stalling and pay the money. I'm done. I want out.

Besides, it's not like the police are jumping through hoops to try to obtain evidence or information. If I want to know where they're at in the case, I have to call them to find out. They never call us. They never followed up with Nathan's wife, and that makes me think they don't give a rat's ass.

The café is crowded, and I weave my way through the front tables, keeping my head down, my eyes searching for Nathan. He's tucked into a dark corner of the room, huddled down in a booth, dressed in black, too. Everything about his demeanor screams paranoid or shifty. By trying to be inconspicuous, he's even more conspicuous. Going through this with him has been a nightmare. It's safe to say my crush on him is officially over after seeing how little common sense he has. I feel like I've made most of the sensible decisions throughout this process. But I guess he at least can get his hands on some money.

I step closer to the booth and clear my throat. "Nathan."

He tosses a glance at me over his shoulder, nods, and gestures to the empty seat across from him.

I slide into the booth seat. "It was a trek to get here. Traffic was hell."

"Sorry," Nathan says, keeping his gaze directed toward the table. There's only a glass of water in front of him, and it's beading with condensation.

I clasp my hands in my lap and cross my legs, leaning forward, speaking in a low voice. "What do we do from here?"

Nathan's upper lip twitches, and he doesn't respond right away. This is how I know he's about to drop a bombshell on me.

"I've been taking money from the company for a while now," he says.

I'm not surprised. I shake my head. "For how long?"

"A while. Angela shops, you know?"

I could roll my eyes. Of course, he'd blame his stealing on his wife's spending habits. *Jesus, why did I ever sleep with this cretin?*

"Anyway," he continues. "I have about five thousand

stored up now in an offshore account. And I can get five from our savings."

"You already have five grand from the company?"

Nathan has dark circles under his eyes as he slowly lifts his head and nods twice. "Yes." The vacant expression on his face gives nothing away.

"I thought you said you were going to *try* to get some money from the company. I didn't know you'd already done it. When?"

Nathan scratches his jawline, not meeting my gaze. "A couple months."

"A couple—Nathan, a couple *months*?" I hiss.

He nods again, staring at me like a child anticipating a scolding.

"Nathan, why didn't you tell me? I could have given it to the blackmailer already."

He scowls. "It's still not enough to give them."

"Yeah, but at least it would have been something. It could've kept them at bay at least or have worked as a partial payment. I might have been able to sleep at night, Nathan." Heat spreads through my veins. "Look at me. I've lost weight over this. I've made myself sick, and you've been sitting on this... on this money all this time!"

Hot tears sting my eyes, and my chin quivers. I will myself not to cry in front of this arrogant, self-serving jerk, but it's difficult to keep my emotions in check.

"I'm sorry." Nathan's face crumbles.

He seems sincere—I'll give him that—but it does little to reassure me. I'm pissed, and I can't hold back. My face is scalding hot, my blood is boiling, and my heart runs at a hundred miles an hour.

"Where were you when I was the only one being targeted?

You had the money, and you wouldn't help. You told me to ignore it."

"That was before things escalated," Nathan argues, his eyes pleading, his tone defensive.

A family of four walks past us to a neighboring booth. The mother holds a babbling infant, and the father is trying to get his toddler to walk in a straight line. I stare at the table and take measured breaths.

"I'm furious at you for defrauding the company, too."

"You can't have it both ways, Lucy," he says in a singsong voice. "Taking the money means you're defrauding the company, too."

I chew on my bottom lip and bounce my leg under the table, stewing.

"You and I both know we still need to pay the blackmailer, and even the measly five thousand is chump change in comparison to what we *still* would owe," he says. "But at least it's a fucking start."

I park my elbows on the table and cradle my head in my hands. "I know. You're right." I take a deep breath and settle into a calmer demeanor, glancing at Nathan across the table. "I called my dad. He said he'll loan me ten thousand."

Nathan leans into the back of the booth and exhales through parted lips. The relief on his face is instant. He regards me as though an idea has just clicked on in his brain. "Do you have paper and a pen in your purse?"

"Yeah, why?"

"I want the blackmailer's number."

"Why can't you store it on your phone?"

Nathan shakes his head. "I don't want it on my phone."

Sighing, I reach into my purse and draw out a pen and paper from a small notepad I carry around with me. I pull up the number from my phone and recite it to Nathan as he scribbles it down. He folds the paper in half and shoves it deep into his hoodie pocket.

Then he stands up abruptly, glancing down at me. "I'll be in touch with the blackmailer. I'll get information on how to make the money transfer."

I nod. No matter how much I hate Nathan now, we're in this together. The steely determination on his face reflects how I feel. This is it. The end. I hope.

24

There it is. Ten thousand dollars in my bank account, transferred from my dad. Seeing it makes me want to throw up. He asked no questions. He didn't scold me. He simply sent me what I asked for. My innocent father has no idea the real reason I needed this money, and it shatters my soul to be so deceptive.

Hopefully, he'll never have to find out, and I can work out a payment plan to get the money back to him. But I need to focus on one problem at a time, the current one being how to get the money to the blackmailer.

"How do they want it?" I ask Nathan in the break room at work. We're alone, but we don't know how long that may last, so we need to keep this conversation short and productive.

Nathan rubs his finger under his nose. "Cash."

I sigh. "Okay. I don't know if the bank will let me withdraw that much."

"Most have a 10K limit, so you should be fine. You could get five today and five tomorrow if it's a problem."

"I'll go to the bank on my lunch break—"

"No, Lucy, you need to do it now." Nathan pushes off from the counter, urgency swimming in his eyes. He tosses a paranoid glance past me to the break room door. "I'll cover for you. If anyone asks, I'll say you had an appointment or something. Don't worry—I'll keep it vague."

I swallow down a huge knot of fear that's been stubbornly wedged in my throat and nod. "All right. I'll go now."

I wish Nathan could go with me, but I understand why he can't. He can't be caught with me by any security cameras. And we don't want to give the blackmailer any extra ways to fuck with us or push us deeper into the dirt.

"Call me when you get back to the office," Nathan says. "I'll meet you in the parking lot by your car."

"Okay."

"Lucy?" His expression is guarded, his eyes narrow. "Are you understanding?"

"Yes," I croak. "Why?"

He takes a step away to widen the gap between us. "It looked like you were in a daze or something, like you couldn't really hear what I was saying."

I rub my temples to quell some of the intense pounding from my massive migraine. "This is a lot to handle."

Nathan's features soften. "I know it's overwhelming and scary right now, but it's almost over."

"I hope you're right," I say as I walk out.

⌐

Two hours later, I'm in the parking lot, sitting in my car, waiting for Nathan to meet me. The ten thousand dollars is burning a hole through the passenger seat, where it sits in a manila envelope. Getting it was bizarre. I'm still sweating through my shirt. The amount raised some questions among the bank staff, and there were certain reporting requirements. But I stuck to my story that the money was for a large purchase from a person who didn't trust banks. I told them I was buying a horse. My dad's recent transfer helped. I think Daddy buying his daughter a pony made the teller want to roll his eyes rather than report me to the government for suspicious behavior. I hope my nerves weren't on show.

Soon, Nathan approaches. It's a drizzly day, and mist collects in his hair, like little beads of translucent glitter.

I roll down the window, and his eyes skim to the passenger seat and he nods toward the envelope. "That's it?"

I reach for it and hand it to him. Nathan's eyes pan left and right to make sure no one is in plain sight, watching, then shoves the envelope into his briefcase.

"I'm going to meet the blackmailer now."

"Nathan, wait." I almost reach for his hand, but I don't. It doesn't feel appropriate after he lied to me.

He stares at me expectantly. "What?"

"Nothing. Just be careful. This needs to end."

Nathan's face is stoic. He gives me a swift nod and backs away from the car. "Once it's done, I'll send you a message."

"Okay."

Nathan turns around as if he has an afterthought he needs to share. "I told everyone I sent you home for the day because you weren't feeling well, so don't go back to the office. Go home and lock all the doors. Wait for contact from me."

"Got it," I say, cranking my engine as I roll up the window. I don't pull out of the parking lot until I see him leave.

At home, I can't eat. I can't sleep. I chew my nails. I pace. I wring my hands. I stare out my front and back windows. I pull up the security camera footage a dozen times and check my phone about a dozen more.

There's nothing. Radio silence. I haven't heard from Nathan at all, and it's been hours. He promised to let me know when the deal was done.

Did something go wrong? Did he follow through? Is he hurt?

The worst-case scenarios slither through my brain, sprout wings, and take flight. I picture Nathan's lifeless body soaked in rain on the sidewalk. Blood seeps from his corpse. I pace half the night and sleep restlessly the other half.

By the time the morning comes, I've tossed and turned for three hours and drank four cups of coffee. Still no word from Nathan. I rub my sore eyes. It's gone wrong. I can feel it.

I type out a text to him.

Everything okay?

It's vague enough to not give anything away, but Nathan will understand it.

No response.

The only thing I can do is head into work like nothing has happened. I brush my teeth, apply makeup, pull my hair into a bun, and don a smart dress. If something has happened to Nathan, I need to think about a contingency plan. Do I go straight to the police, or do I pretend like nothing has happened and carry on as normal? If I opt for the latter, I can at least check that Nathan isn't ghosting me. Surely, he'd turn up at work. On the other hand, if he is dead, at least I'm doing the things I normally do. Not turning up might be a red flag.

After all, I have no alibi for last night. And that could be an issue.

My legs shake as I walk into the office. I nod a hello in Chet's direction. Janine hurries in a few moments after me, slightly late as always. I am barely on time today. She heads straight to Nathan's office and knocks on the door. From the other side of the room, I watch carefully.

She knocks a second time then opens the door. "Nathan?"

She shakes her head and closes the door. My heart pounds. Nathan isn't in his office. I try to open my inbox, hoping to not make it too obvious that I'm watching Janine. She walks into the break room and straight back out.

He's not here. I know it. I just know it.

Chet walks over to Nathan's office and knocks. Then he approaches Janine, and they have a conversation. Janine scrolls through something on the computer.

At this point, I can't stand it. I walk over to them. "Is Nathan in?"

Chet shakes his head. "We were supposed to be meeting, but he hasn't turned up."

"Check the men's bathroom," Janine suggests.

"No chance," Chet says. "I'm not interrupting a man's business."

"Well, see if one of the stalls is closed," she says, shooing him away.

Chet returns a few minutes later and shakes his head. "He's not in there."

"I'd better call his wife," Janine says, grabbing the receiver.

I take a step away from the desk, not wanting to hear Angela's voice on the other line. Chet walks over and stands next to me.

"Maybe he's sick," Chet says. "Bit weird, though, isn't it?"

"Yeah," I say, chewing on a thumbnail.

"Did he mention any new clients or anything to you?" he asks. "Was he meeting anyone yesterday?"

I turn to Chet, eyeballing him. "What do you mean?"

Chet shrugs. "Maybe he's keeping something under wraps—that's all. He's been acting strangely recently."

Behind us, Janine replaces the phone receiver with a clunk. "So, turns out Nathan didn't go home last night. His wife is about to file a missing person report."

25

When I stumble back to my desk, I feel like I'm walking through molasses. Thank God I didn't have to speak to Angela on the phone. I'm not sure how I'd cope. Guilt gnaws away at my stomach. *A missing person report.* I check my phone. Nothing from Nathan. Nothing from the blackmailer. My neck is clammy with heat, but my hands feel cold.

Nathan's kids could be without a father. The thought makes me dizzy. My limbs want to move, but my body is heavy. I snatch up my desk phone, find a card for Officer Calypso, and call.

"Calypso," she answers.

"It's Lucy Croft."

"Good morning, Ms. Croft. Like I said last time, I'll drop you a call when I have any more infor—"

"Actually, I'm the one with the information."

"You are? You'd better tell me what that is, then." I hear her working her jaw, still chewing her gum.

"Nathan went to meet the blackmailer last night, and he

didn't come home. His wife just filed a missing person report."

"Why would he meet the blackmailer?" Calypso asks.

I hesitate before I answer, knowing this doesn't sound good. "We raised the cash. All 20K. He was going to the drop-off point."

There's a heavy sigh on the other end of the phone. "You're going to have to come in."

I don't bother making up a decent excuse. I tell Chet I have an appointment with a client and then leave the office. On the way out, I notice Vivian isn't at her desk. And then I wonder if I saw her that morning. I was so wrapped up in the black-mailing drama I didn't notice. But if she was there before, I wonder what she might have heard me say on the phone. Maybe she's on leave, and I'm overthinking it.

It's almost two by the time I reach the station. I can't say I enjoyed the journey. Now that Nathan is gone, I can only assume I'm next. Maybe this has never been about money. Maybe it's about murder. Revenge. My eyes dart up to the rearview mirror as I sit in the parking lot, willing myself to move. Every car is a potential stalker.

Officer Calypso has arranged a meeting between me and the detective who has taken over the case. She told me over the phone that she'll escort me to the conference room and will attend the meeting with me if I wish. I do wish. A familiar face might make this more bearable.

She's waiting in the lobby, not chewing gum, for a change. We exchange nods as a way of greeting, neither of us smiling but not unfriendly to each other either.

"Afternoon, Ms. Croft," she says. "This is Detective Andrew Higgins. He's the lead on this case now, though I'll be here as a liaison if needed, seeing as I took the call to your house the other night."

"Right," I say, trying to take it all in.

Detective Higgins pumps my palm. He's broad shouldered and stocky with a gentle smile and brown eyes that hold my gaze confidently without seeming cocky.

"Nice to meet you," he says. "You can follow us this way, and we'll go have a conversation."

Conversation. I like the sound of that. It's not an interrogation. We're simply going to talk. But then I consider that this might be a tactic employed by the police to put their suspects at ease. *Suspects.* No one has called me that, I remember. Just myself in my own mind as I imagine the worst.

We make our way through to a meeting room, and they seat me at the table. Officer Calypso takes a seat next to me while Detective Higgins crosses to the other side. It's subtle, but I can tell they're trying to make me feel as though someone is on my side. My defenses rise. *Should I have hired a lawyer?*

"Coffee?" Higgins asks.

I shake my head. I have enough caffeine running through my veins as it is.

He smiles, tapping his pen against a notepad. Then he leans forward and points to the corner of the room. "Now, I want to let you know right off the bat that there is a camera in here recording audio and video, but you're not in any trouble. This isn't an interrogation. Just a chat. Okay?"

"Okay." I'm not sure I believe him about it being simply a chat. "Where do you want me to start?"

"At the beginning if you like." Detective Higgins's smile

comes across as genuine. He's wearing a lanyard around his neck with his picture and security clearance information.

I start to tell them everything, little by little. It gets easier as the words flow, but occasionally, Officer Calypso hands me a tissue. I confess about the affair, about how we had sex in the car. I tell them about how afterward, strange things started happening, about how we were getting threatening texts and picture evidence of us being intimate together. They already knew about the bracelet package, of course.

When I'm finished, I lean back in the chair, spent. My throat hurts from talking so much. I feel vulnerable and exposed but also free and relieved that it's all out in the open and the police have all the nightmarish details.

They don't judge me. They don't scream at me or belittle me. They don't back me into a corner with manipulative question tactics. They listen and offer advice after I'm done spilling everything to them.

Detective Higgins scratches the side of his head with the top of his pen. "We did see the missing person report his wife filed, but something still isn't adding up here."

"Like what?"

"Well, for starters, Nathan is a grown man. He's only been missing twenty-four hours, if he's even missing at all. Adults can leave of their own free will. They don't have to tell anyone where they're going."

"Are you saying that you think he left on purpose?"

Detective Higgins exchanges a glance with Officer Calypso. "I can't say for sure without evidence of him being abducted by someone. We can pull cameras in the area around your office and his house, but I can't say with absolute certainty that we'll find anything."

"It's something you can try, though?"

"Absolutely."

I stare at the table, dumbfounded by this new development and Detective Higgins's impression of the case. I can't imagine Nathan wanting to leave on purpose. Then again, part of me believes I need to consider it. After all, Nathan was carrying thousands of dollars when he disappeared.

"So, you think he could've taken the money and run?" My hands ball into fists. "Oh my God. Was it him? Did he do this?"

I'm not sure what's worse, Nathan orchestrating all this or leaving me to deal with a blackmailer on my own. Or the possibility that the blackmailer killed him and now I have a violent stalker following me.

Detective Higgins considers me as if he's choosing his next words carefully. "Again, I can't be certain, but it's a theory. He might be hiding out for a few days, trying to figure out a different way to get himself out of a bad situation."

"What do I do now?" I ask.

"Go home, go back to your life, and try your best to keep your routine as normal as possible."

"How can I do that with a blackmailer on the loose and Nathan missing? How do I know I'm safe at home?" I find my gaze meeting Calypso's, pleading with my eyes. This isn't going in the direction I thought it would. They barely seem concerned.

"We can have an officer escort you home if you'd like," Higgins says.

"To stay with me there?"

He frowns. "Unfortunately, we don't have those kinds of resources on hand right now, but if you feel unsafe or see anything suspicious, then don't hesitate to give us a call."

"Wh-What if he's dead?" I say. "If he's been murdered, I could be next."

"We don't think that's what happened here," the detective says. "Frankly, Ms. Croft, Nathan Robertson was in a troubled marriage and a lot of debt. He embezzled money from the company. This sounds much more likely to be the sick plan of a man who wants out of his life. I'm sorry you got pulled into this, Ms. Croft, but it seems very likely that he conned you out of the money, added it to the money he's already stolen, and left to start a new life somewhere. I'm so sorry."

I lean back in my chair, floored. "You really think so?"

"It's not unheard-of," Calypso adds. "I've seen people do some crazy shit to get out of a marriage."

"What about Angela?" I ask. "Does she know this?"

"We've talked to her," Higgins says. "She knows everything we knew up to that point."

"So she knows about the affair?"

"Yes."

"I guess it's the least of her problems now," I mutter.

"I'm sorry there isn't more we can do for you. I wish we could give you a different answer." Detective Higgins stands up and rebuttons his blazer. The meeting is over. There's nothing left for me to do. "We'll be in touch." He escorts me to the door. "But in the meantime, let us know if you want an officer to follow you to your residence."

"No, it's fine."

If their theories are correct, I'm not in any danger now. And what's the point of having a cop follow me home if they aren't going to guard my property anyway? I can't help thinking about how I conned ten grand from my dad. When I climb into the driver's seat of my car, a flash of red-hot rage hits my veins. I pound the steering wheel so hard the horn goes off, and a few passersby turn to stare at me. I mouth, "Fuck off," to someone, and they quickly look away.

It's Nathan I want to tell to fuck off. I remember his hands on me back at the hotel. I remember the rush of adrenaline I felt. If only I could turn back time and get him out of my life.

26

Detective Higgins said to carry on as normal. My plan was to quit my job and move back home. But if I quit right away and something has happened to Nathan, it might make me appear guilty. So I take the detective's advice, and I go in to work the next day. I shuffle to my cubicle when Chet comes around a corner, carrying a cup of coffee.

He stops when he sees me, his eyes wide with concern. "Wow. You look rough."

I give him a weak smirk because it's all I can muster. It's too early in the morning for me to deal with his humor. "Thanks, Chet. You sure know how to compliment a woman."

I try to squeeze past him, but he puts his arm on the wall to keep me from going around him. I look at him then his arm, contemplating ducking under it.

"I didn't mean it," he says.

"That's a world-class apology."

"Sorry. Have you heard anything about Nathan?"

"No, you?"

He shakes his head. "But to add to the weirdness, Vivian called in sick this morning."

"What?" I give him a cautious glance. Vivian never calls in sick. I once saw her come into the office so out of it with the flu, she could barely walk. Nathan sent her home, but it showed her loyalty to the firm. I've never been that sort of martyr myself—I'd rather not spread germs around—but she took her work that seriously.

"And no offense..." Chet grins and raises his arms by his sides. "But you look like you haven't slept in a week."

I swallow hard and try to brush past him again now that his arm gate is gone. "I've had some issues with sleeping lately, yes." I don't turn around to address him as I walk away.

"Guilty conscience?"

I don't want to ask him what he means, but I know I have to. Slowly, turning on my heel, I face him. "What?"

"Janine told me. I guess that's one way to get a promotion."

"Fuck you, Chet," I say, walking away.

The atmosphere in the office is unsettled. We're down two, and Chet doesn't seem to be interested in doing any actual work. He hangs out in the break room instead. Even Janine is quiet. She's staring out into space, her eyes unfocused. And then I realize she isn't wearing any makeup. Not a single ounce. Not even blush. Janine comes to work every single day with about a pound of makeup caked on her face. Her hair hasn't been brushed, and there are dark circles beneath her eyes. I walk over to her desk.

She blinks. "Hey, girl. You okay?"

"Hey, Janine. I'm okay. What about you?" I make sure I sound more concerned than curious.

"Uh-huh."

I'm not convinced, but I don't press her. It's scary for your boss to go missing. That might be why Vivian is off sick, too. Maybe she doesn't want to sit here and stare at Nathan's empty office. I'm surprised Lucas Weathers hasn't been down to give us a pep talk or work with us until Nathan's back.

He's not coming back. If Detective Higgins is right, Nathan is out there somewhere, carving out a new life. But what if the detective is wrong?

I lower myself into my chair and shake my computer mouse to wake up my screen. I force myself to get some work done or, at the very least, distract myself with the accounts that I currently have. I have at least fifty emails to respond to, so it's a promising start.

However, I don't get very far into my neglected work. The Financial Crime Unit of the FBI comes into the office around lunchtime. They don't make a scene. It's not like in the movies where they ambush the place and swarm everywhere, screaming in people's faces, guns blazing. They are quiet, discreet, as they slip into Nathan's office and close the door to conduct an investigation since I blew his cover about the embezzlement.

Janine regards me. I slink deeper in my chair and hide my face behind my computer screen. I have no regrets. I just want them to find Nathan. And my money. And the blackmailer, if it isn't Nathan. We all deserve an explanation at this point. What we've been through isn't fair. If this all was Nathan, he needs to be held accountable.

I use the lunchtime excuse to leave the office. The place is stifling and depressing. It's like Nathan vacuumed the life out of the place when he stole money and disappeared. Back in the fresh air, I can breathe. A magpie flutters past me. Then I see a face emerge from an SUV.

Anyone but her. My brain tries to find a way for me to get out of what's coming next, but she's already clocked me and runs over. We make eye contact, so now I have no choice but to wait for her.

She halts in front of me, a little out of breath from trying to chase me down. I bristle, not wanting to look her in the eye. But I don't want to act like a coward, so I force myself to do it and try to pacify my thrashing heart.

"Hey, Angela."

"Hey, Lucy."

We stare at each other, neither of us speaking. The silence feels like it drudges on for an eternity.

"Do you know?" I say, barely above a whisper.

She nods. "The police thought it best to show me the threatening messages Nathan received. I... saw the photo... of you both together."

Guilt washes over me like freezing cold water. "I'm sorry. I never meant to hurt your family. I swear."

Angela's face flinches, but she nods. "I'm not here to yell and scream at you. I need to talk to you about something important in a civilized, adult way. Can you agree to that?"

I swallow hard. Her reaction unnerves me. "Yes. But I... I guess I don't know what you want." At this point, I feel so ashamed, so thoroughly guilt-ridden that I think I might agree to anything she asks.

Angela gives me a look as if she can't understand who I am as a person. I'm still trying to figure that one out myself.

"I don't care about the affair, Lucy."

"You don't?"

"I just want to find Nathan," she says.

"The police are handling it," I assure her. "I'm not sure what else we can do. They're the professionals."

Angela cuts her gaze away from me, turning toward the building where we work. Her eyes stop at the windows of our office floor. "There are things you don't know, Lucy. Personal things between me and Nathan. He has a gambling addiction."

"Fuck." I sigh. "Do the police know?"

She nods. "He's raked up a huge amount of debt. I think he's run off with the money you gave him."

"The detective said the same thing. But I didn't know about the gambling. I didn't realize his debts were that bad. I'm so sorry, Angela. I guess he's gone for good, probably in fucking—I don't know, Aruba or something."

"You might be right. But I don't know for sure. He might be in trouble with someone he owes money to. It's all messed up. I'm worried that something happened to him. I feel like he'd check in with me if he ran off. I think he's in trouble. Call it a wife's intuition, but he needs help. He could be hurt, dying, trapped somewhere. He could be tied to a chair with a gun held to his head." Her shoulders hitch as she tries to hold back a sob. "I know he's weak, and that he's done awful things. I know all that. But he's the father of my children. The kids want their daddy back." Angela covers her face with her hands and weeps.

"Okay, okay." I give her an apprehensive pat on the back.

I feel sorry for her—I do. She seems miserable. I'm part of the reason her life has been turned upside down, and I'm shackled with the guilt of it. But I also can't help wondering if the little boy Nathan created a faux kidnapping with might be better off without his father.

"Angela, please stop crying. I'll—fuck. I'll help you find him, okay? We'll find him. Everything will work out. Just please stop crying."

27

I follow Angela's car to her home, which is pretty much exactly what I pictured, tucked in at the bottom of a quiet cul-de-sac with ivy climbing up two porch columns that frame a red door. An oak tree in the front yard has a tire swing hanging from the lowest branch. Perhaps it's the tree, but it reminds me of my own childhood home. A pang of homesickness hits me, and I hope that soon I'll be able to leave and start again.

Angela leads me inside to a decor scheme that could rival something in a designer magazine. Everything is white, airy, and bright. Her furniture could be brand new. Maybe Nathan wasn't exaggerating about her spending habits, not that it justifies anything he did.

"Would you like a glass of wine?" she asks.

I exhale slowly, giving in to the temptation. "Sure. Why not." Things are so awkward with Angela that I need to loosen up a bit. "Only one, though. I'm driving."

"Of course." She sniffs and rubs her red eyes as she heads to the kitchen. "I'll be right back. Make yourself at home."

This is beyond strange. I'm in the house of my boss, who I slept with and who then possibly stole my money and ran away from his life and responsibilities. A few weeks ago, I suspected Angela might be behind all of this. But I underestimated how morally bankrupt Nathan is. I can't shake that niggle deep down that there's more going on than there seems to be. And maybe, just maybe, Angela is right about Nathan being in trouble. If that's the case, I owe it to her and their kids to help.

I'm about to take a seat on the white sofa, when a thought pops into my head. It wasn't long ago that I found Angela suspicious. She could have been the one to send the messages and she sat next to me at the awards ceremony which meant she could steal my jewelry.

Concerned, I make my way into the kitchen, just in time to watch her pour the wine. She pours two glasses, both from the same bottle, and hands me one. I wait for a moment, until she takes a sip.

"Thank you again for agreeing to come here and help me," she says. "I realize how weird this must be for you."

"It's pretty weird," I admit.

She takes another sip of wine. "Yeah, I know. But you know so much about what's been going on that I knew I needed to talk to you. If... well, I guess I'll do anything I can to make this situation better. It's been so hard on me and the kids."

"Where are the kids?" I glance around the living room, noticing for the first time how quiet it is.

"They're at my sister's house. She's been a big help to me ever since..." Angela trails off, tearing up. "And I didn't want them around because it's hard for them. You know? Seeing the empty house without Nathan in it." She takes another drink of her wine.

I begin to relax. Surely the wine can't be drugged if I saw her pour two glasses from the same bottle and watch her drink from one of them. We head into the lounge and take a seat on her sofa.

"Angela——" I start.

"No, don't say anything." Angela cuts me off and raises a hand. "I probably brought it on myself."

"Why would you say that? You didn't make him steal from the company or..." I was about to say *make him sleep with me*, but I can't bring myself to utter the words out loud. "Angela, I'm so sorry for all the pain I've caused you. That's why I'm here now. I want to tell you everything that's been happening and how we got to this fucked-up moment in time. I want to help you find Nathan and bring him back to his family, where he belongs."

"Right. That's what I want." She sniffs. "The kids have been asking where their daddy is, and I don't know how to answer."

At this point, I could use a whole bottle of wine, and I suspect that Angela needs a shoulder to cry on more than she wants to do detective work. Or maybe she simply wanted to meet me face-to-face, the woman who slept with her husband.

"Can I ask you a question?" she asks.

"Yes," I say, bracing myself.

"How many times did you sleep with my husband?"

It knocks the air from my lungs. So this is it. She wants answers. "Twice. Both times happened at the work retreat we went to. Nothing happened afterward, I promise you. We had to deal with the blackmail, and we talked because of that, but there wasn't anything between us anymore." My wine glass is half-empty already, but I take another sip.

Angela nods and stares at her lap. "That's when I noticed he was acting funny."

"I had too much to drink that first night. But it's still no excuse. The second time, it was after we'd argued. It was an intense moment in the car. I guess we let the pressure and the tension get the better of us." I pause. "My mom died a few months before I went on the retreat, and I'm not trying to justify my behavior, but I was in a vulnerable place. I think I latched onto Nathan as some way to... to get some human contact, you know? I don't know what I'm trying to say."

"I think I understand." Her eyes drift over to the window. "It's not the first time Nathan's been unfaithful to me."

"It's not?" My delivery is flat because I'm not in the slightest bit surprised.

"About a year after the twins were born, Nathan strayed with another woman he met at a bar. I chose to forgive him because he was crying and distraught at the time. He used the excuse that the kids were a lot to handle and he was stressed out and needed a break. He told me he wasn't thinking clearly." Angela is quiet, gazing into her wine glass with a pensive expression. "I took him back because I could relate. Carson and Madeleine were tough to manage back then. They are still a lot of work. I wanted to give him and our marriage another chance because I loved him."

She uses the word *love* in the past tense. I can't help but pick up on that. He betrayed her for a second time, not just by sleeping with me but by stealing money too. I would find it hard to continue to love a man like Nathan.

"That doesn't give him the right to do what he did," I say.

Angela nods. Nathan sold her short. He painted a picture

of this frenzied wife who was always on his back, nagging him, who wouldn't calm down or give him space to breathe. But she isn't like that at all. She seems reasonable—too forgiving if anything.

"I was too hard on him." Angela shakes her head, her eyes pinching closed. Her tone is grim. "I'm the one who pushed him away."

"Holy shit, Angela. Are you insane? He's the bad guy here. It's not your fault Nathan couldn't handle his own problems in his life. If you ask me, they weren't even problems to start with. He has two beautiful, healthy children. He has a wonderful home and a gorgeous, supportive wife that he honestly doesn't deserve. He has—well, had—a stable job. What else could he possibly need?" Maybe it's the wine, but I'm done tiptoeing around Nathan's bad behavior. "Now is my chance to make it up to you. For everything I've done wrong." I cup my hand over hers and give her a collaborative smile. "If you'll let me."

Angela doesn't slip her hand away from mine. Instead, she gives me a heartfelt smile. "If I didn't want to give you the chance to make it up to me, then I wouldn't have let you in my house."

I swipe at a rogue tear rolling down my face. "Yes, I suppose that's true."

I'm at the bottom of my wine glass. Angela asks me if I'd like another. The alcohol runs through my veins, making me feel warm. Some of the tension has lifted from my body.

"Yes, another couldn't hurt. Thank you." Maybe I won't drive home right away. I'll stay with her for a bit. She's so alone here.

Angela returns with another glass for me and for her. She sets them down and clasps her hands together. "Enough apologies and tears. I brought you here to help, so let's get into it."

We dig deeper into the case, discussing theories of what could have happened to Nathan. Nothing is off the table for Angela. She's stoic as we talk about the possibility of Nathan being dead. I drain my wine, my face warm. After a while, my mind starts to feel foggy. It's probably a combination of the wine, the stress of the confession, and the lack of sleep.

"I've had too much to drink, I think."

Angela frowns. "We drained almost two bottles."

"Did we?" She's no longer in focus. "Two bottles? I thought... I only had two glasses, didn't I?" The room spins. How long have I been in this house? I thought it was about an hour or so, but now it seems longer. My head feels like it weighs a hundred pounds. "I think I need to go home and rest."

When I try to lift myself from the couch, Angela clamps a sturdy hand over my shoulder and gives me a concerned glance.

"I don't think you should drive tonight, Lucy. You can stay in our guest room if you like."

"Really?"

"Yes, of course. I wouldn't want you to get behind the wheel and endanger yourself or someone else. We have enough going on right now to worry about someone else getting hurt."

She's so kind. I think I say that out loud, but I'm not sure. Maybe I think it instead. We can't be friends—I realize that. But Angela has been patient and civil with me. Her smile is sincere. I'm weak, and my head is cloudy. I don't have enough energy to protest.

"Okay, if you're sure."

"Absolutely." Angela's lips splinter into a smile. It's the last thing I see before my eyelids droop and shut.

⌐

I've always hated waking up in a different bed—the subtle differences in how the mattress feels, the scent of someone else's detergent on the sheets. Even the light filters in through the window in a different way. It's usually because of curtains that don't close quite right or move in the breeze.

The morning after going to Angela's house, I wake to new scents and sensations, as I expected. But what I didn't expect is the festering stench of mold, the cold cement beneath my body, and the fact that I'm in utter darkness and can't lift my arms.

I sit up straight. Adrenaline wakes me up sharp. Confusion sharpens into reality. I'm shackled somehow. Handcuffs maybe. I might be in a basement. My head throbs, and my throat is dry. I've been drugged. I'm slowly coming around from a deep, deep slumber. My muscles ache, especially my neck, which must have been at a weird angle given the hard floor.

Last night, Angela smiled at me as she gave me wine. She'd told me all about how we could move on and that she forgave me. But now I'm trapped. This is it. This is my punishment.

28

The air shifts, and there's a scrape across the cement. A body stirs next to me, and when I feel a tug on my arm, I try to scuttle away. Whatever—whoever—it is jerks forward with me, and I realize we're cuffed together. Their face emerges from the shadows, and it takes me a moment to figure out who this familiar shape is.

Then I flatten myself against the wall, a soft whimper coming from my throat. *What if he's in on it?*

"Lucy?" Nathan asks. "Is it you?"

"It's me. What are you doing here?" I keep still. My hands ball into fists, ready to protect myself, not that I can do much in the cuffs.

"Angela. I think it was her."

"She drugged me. Do you know where we are?"

He shakes his head, his expression dazed. "I have no idea."

I scream. It's involuntary, and I can't stop. At first, Nathan's eyes skid across me as if I've lost my mind. Then he joins in.

"Help!" I yell. "Help us. Please!"

And then we stop. We listen.

"There's no one here," Nathan says. "I think we're in some sort of shelter. Like a tornado shelter or something."

"Is it always this dark, or is it nighttime?"

"Wait," he says, reaching for a string above our heads.

A single lightbulb baths the room in yellow light. I get my first real view of our prison. We're in a concrete room. The walls are bare. There's no furniture, no food. It's cramped, too. Nathan is right—it appears to be a storm shelter. If that's true, it means we must be away from the city, in a rural area.

"This can't be happening," I say. "It can't be real. I'm... Tell me this is a nightmare."

"I wish I could," he replies.

"Have you been here this whole time? Since you went missing?"

He nods.

I shake my head. "I can't believe it. I know I said long ago that the blackmailer could be your wife. But it wasn't until she slipped that drug into my drink that I truly understood what she was capable of. I'm scared, Nathan. This is revenge. Pure revenge." I stare at the handcuffs then at Nathan. He's oddly quiet, and he won't meet my gaze. He seems shifty, like he knows more than he lets on. "Just tell me, Nathan. Whatever it is you're holding back, tell me. If we're going to get out of here alive, we're going to have to work together." He's still quiet. "Nathan!"

"All right. All right." He leans back against the wall and closes his eyes. "Angela didn't blackmail anyone."

I sigh. "So it was you all this time." He's silent again. "Nathan, tell me the truth. All of it."

"It's complicated."

"Well, apparently, we have plenty of time. So we might as well get to it."

Nathan takes a deep, shaky breath. "I took the money. I fucking *stole* it, okay? It was me. I'm a fucking asshole, and I blackmailed you, faked everything, and stole the money."

I'm unmoved by his discomfort as he owns up to his crimes. "Why?"

Nathan tunnels his fingers through his hair with his free hand and lets out a groan of angst. "I had to."

"Why?" I shove him. "How could you do this to me?"

Nathan's eyes are fixed on the floor. "It was a setup to scam you out of money. You're an easy target. You live alone, you recently lost your mom, so you're vulnerable and easy to scare. And... well, you don't usually break rules, but I knew you had a crush on me. I figured if we had an affair, you'd be racked with guilt and comply with everything I said."

What he's telling me cuts deep because it's all true. But I don't have time to become defeated or self-conscious about the decisions I've already made. "Why were you embezzling money from the company, then, if it was so easy to steal from me?"

"It started out with the embezzling," he admits. "I got in over my head with it. I had stolen quite a bit."

"More than five thousand?"

Nathan pauses then slowly nods.

"Someone must have helped you."

Nathan says nothing. I watch him for ten, maybe twenty seconds. Someone at the company must have helped him. *Janine? Chet? Vivian?*

Then it hits me. One person phoned in sick the day the FBI turned up to search Nathan's office. "Vivian."

Nathan raises his chin, and the truth is written on his face, plain as day. I'm right.

"She'd been helping me with the wire frauds and getting the money into offshore accounts," Nathan admits.

"Where is she now? Wait, are we definitely sure it was Angela who did this to us? I was at her house when I went to sleep, but what if Vivian orchestrated this somehow? Your kids weren't with Angela when I went over to your house." I suddenly remember she hadn't explained that and I'd forgotten to ask. "I went to see if I could help her find you." I roll my eyes. "Even though the police told me they thought you'd run off with the money, I was still prepared to give you the benefit of the doubt. But what if Vivian saw me at Angela's and broke in somehow..." I trail off. It doesn't fit together.

Nathan shakes his head. "Vivian and I were... are... in love. We have been for a long time. We wanted this money to start a new life together. She had no reason to do this. But Angela, on the other hand..." He raises his eyebrows.

I let that sink in because the Vivian I know and the Nathan I know make a really weird combination. But clearly, neither is what they seem. Then I pull myself back to the situation. Something isn't adding up.

"Angela would need help to pull this off," I say. "She couldn't have done this on her own. I guess she could move me around if she needed to, but not you."

He nods. "I think you're right." Then he leans back against the wall and sighs. "What has she done to Viv? I just... I'm worried, Lucy."

"I think maybe we need to concentrate on getting out of here first. Tell me everything you remember before you woke up in this room."

"I remember getting really sleepy. I was at the house to see the kids one more time before I left with Vivian." He pauses and notices me staring at him. "Don't judge me. I know I'm a piece of shit. But I love my kids."

"Oh, yeah. You love them so much you pretended your own kid was being kidnapped and then decided to leave them for money and another woman."

"I didn't know that was going to happen," he says. "Vivian didn't tell me, okay? But Carson was always safe with Vivian that day."

"She didn't tell you? Wow." I raise my eyebrows. "You were still going to abandon your kids, though."

"I was planning to contact them again somehow. I just needed to get out and straighten myself out. I was a shit dad anyway." He sighs. "Anyway. I fell asleep before I could leave. I think I had an argument with Angela about the kids before I passed out. She poured me a whiskey. I bet she drugged it."

"Yeah, I remember, right before I passed out, thinking it was weird how drunk I felt. I'd only had two glasses. You didn't see anyone else?"

He shakes his head. "No one. Just her. But I guess the question has to be asked. Who helped her? She couldn't do this alone."

I glance at Nathan, who's staring at his feet. We're both thinking it. We don't want to find out who has been helping Angela. Whoever it is has access to a storm shelter and hand-cuffs and can move an unconscious man. We're talking about a hulking man here.

Finally, he speaks. "When we needed to spook you at your apartment, Vivian stole your bracelet at the awards cere-mony. But we didn't have a way to get it to your apartment without giving ourselves an alibi. Vivian suggested we try the dark web. We hired someone to follow you in a truck and deliver the parcel. We... we hired muscle."

"You did *what*?"

I'm disgusted by this man. I yank my arm away, willing the handcuff to break to get me away from him. *Someone from the dark web?* I can only imagine the sleazes who congregate on those sites. And Nathan gave one of them my address.

"I know, it's awful," he says. "We couldn't ask someone we knew to do it because they'd be too suspicious. But I wonder if Angela did the same thing. She's smart enough. I know she's a housewife, and a lot of people think her days are nothing but swimming class and chicken nuggets, but she's always been smart."

"No kidding," I say, gesturing to where we are.

"We're going to be okay. Angela isn't a murderer. She'll call it off. She won't..." His chin wobbles, and he starts to cry.

I hit him on the head. Then I slap his shoulders and his chest. He lets me, all the while pathetically sobbing.

Then I give up and slump against the wall. "Someone will find us. Vivian will figure it out. Or Detective Higgins." But I'm not sure I believe that.

29

After a short while, we work out that we're both strong enough to stand. It takes some balancing, with our wrists connected, but we manage it. We walk over to the storm-shelter door. It's the kind that opens upward so that whoever comes inside can descend the concrete steps. This one is thick and seems heavy. Judging by the hinges, it might be on some sort of hydraulic mechanism to help it open smoothly. Nathan shoves his shoulder against it, but that thing is never going to budge.

He lifts the bottom of his shirt to his face and mops the sweat away from his forehead. He's out of breath, his eyes large and delirious. "It's no use."

"We need to take a break and try again." I refuse to give up. I'm not dying in here next to Nathan. I don't want his face to be the last thing I see.

Nathan shakes his head. "These storm shelters are made to be indestructible. Impenetrable. And God knows where we are. Angela and I don't have a storm shelter at our home. We could be anywhere. We could be in the middle of nowhere or we could be on land owned by whatever kind of psycho Angela enlisted to help her." He sighs. "No one is going to save us. No one is going to hear us scream or bang on that door."

I swallow, my throat dry and raspy. He might be right, but I can't allow us to give up hope. "There has to be a weakness. We have to think everything through. Maybe we wait until someone comes. Surely there'll be someone, right? Angela or whoever she hired. She'll want to see us. Do... something to us."

My free hand rises to my throat. She'll want to murder us. Torture us. I don't know what. The thought is still surreal.

Nathan plants his hands on his hips and assesses the room. He's sweating profusely now, his hair matted to his temples. He looks as frightened as I feel.

"Okay. Okay. We'll figure this out." He sounds like he's trying to convince himself as much as he's trying to convince me, which does little to settle the anxiety churning in my stomach.

"It's so stuffy in here," I say. "No water. No air."

"I know," he says softly. "I feel like that, too. Let's check every nook and cranny. You never know, there might be a weakness. It's not like we're in Fort Knox. This is some prepper's shelter. Maybe it's not as impenetrable as we think."

Together we walk the small room, craning our necks up to the ceiling. Nathan, the tallest by a mile, stands up on his toes, inspecting every surface and corner.

"There has to be a vent," he says. "These places need air circulation."

"I don't know. If there was a vent, wouldn't it be easier to breathe?"

Nathan kneads his fingers into the skin at the back of his

neck. He appears as exhausted as I feel. I slide down the wall and sit with my knees pulled up. The wrist connected to Nathan hangs upright.

"Lucy, get up," he says a moment later.

I lift my head. "No, I'm tired. I need a minute."

He rattles the cuff. "I think I found something."

When I clamber to my feet, he pulls me over to the corner of the wall and points toward the ceiling. Nathan's jaw twitches. "It's a camera."

"Where?"

His hand journeys upward. "Right there."

I follow his finger, and then I see it. The small dark shape that would be easy to miss on a first inspection.

"Fuck," I say. "She's watching us. She and possibly some henchman she hired or her boyfriend or whatever. How sick is that?"

I turn my face away, ashamed and demoralized. *Is this what she wanted—to see us like rats caught in a trap?* I think of us handcuffed together, banging on the door, panicking, walking the perimeter. Tying us up so we couldn't move would have been too boring for her. She wants to watch us squirm.

Nathan jumps, his hand swatting at the camera. It comes off the wall easier than I expected it to. After it hits the ground, Nathan lifts his leg and smashes down on the camera with the heel of his shoe. It makes a crunching noise beneath his weight.

I give him a frantic glance. "Why the hell did you do that? That camera could be our lifeline. We could communicate with our captors."

"If this camera was functioning," Nathan explains, pointing at the broken bits scattered across the floor, "then they'll have to come and check on us, see why the camera stopped working."

It's a theory that could work, but I still have my doubts. "You really think that will make them come back here to check on us?"

"What other option do we have? There's no food or water in here. We're going to lose energy soon. There's no window, no vents. The metal door is reinforced. We'd need a stick of dynamite to blast it off the hinges."

I frown down at the broken pieces of plastic. "I hope you're right about destroying that thing."

Then I shiver, imagining Angela sipping merlot as she watches us. This is a woman who spends her life dropping her kids off at swimming lessons and wiping dirty noses and curling up on the sofa with a glass of merlot to watch *Real Housewives*. At least I thought she was. Clearly, I was way off.

We check the rest of the room for more cameras and then sit back down. My backside hurts from the hard cement floor, but I don't have the energy to stand any longer.

"Lucy," Nathan says. "When, or if, someone comes through that door, we need to be prepared to do anything to get out. *Anything*. Do you understand me?"

"Yes."

"I know we're tired and weak, but you're going to have to let the adrenaline take over because I'm going to run at that motherfucker. All right?"

"Maybe we should have a signal," I suggest.

"Good idea." He gives me some options, and I choose subtle eye contact followed by a loud sniff.

I almost drift off to sleep when we hear a noise by the door. There's scratching at first, then a clicking. The door pops open a crack, and natural light spills into the room. I don't see anyone. The door creaks open an inch wider.

Nathan and I regard each other. He braces himself in a steady position, his hands tightened into fists. He's ready to fight or die trying. I take a deep breath and do the same, stiffening for impact, preparing to defend myself the best way I can.

30

When someone enters the shelter, I expect Angela's slim figure, but instead, a tall, lanky man comes into view. Shadows hide his features until he moves forward, and I realize he's wearing a ski mask. Pale-gray eyes stand out vividly against the dark mask. We remain crouched low, our bodies taut. I have to remind myself to breathe.

The man carries a plastic bag in one hand and opens the door with the other. He closes it behind him and walks down the steps. Then he falters for a moment, his gaze taking in the broken camera. He glances at us and continues his journey down. Through the plastic bag, I can see two bottles of water and what appears to be wrapped sandwiches. I check his other hand for a weapon and see nothing. Then I look at Nathan and wonder what he's considering.

Nathan's glance is furtive. The sniff follows half a second later. I know it's the signal, and I snap up into action, moving with him. With the handcuffs, the motion is trickier than we'd anticipated, and Nathan drags me forward faster than I was prepared for. He lunges at the man, who takes a step back and dumps the bag on the ground. Nathan's arm reaches out for his neck, but the next thing I see is a gun in the masked man's hand.

"Stop!" I yell to Nathan.

He does. He sees it, too. And suddenly Nathan and I back away, returning to the wall.

"Who the hell are you?" Nathan demands.

The gunman says nothing.

"Did my wife put you up to this? What are we doing here?"

I watch Nathan and the masked man carefully. It's clear that Nathan is riled up. His face is flushed and red. He needs to calm down before he gets us killed.

"I want to speak to Angela," Nathan says. "Where is she? Is she behind that door? Fucking answer me!"

As the masked man strides toward us, I raise my free hand to protect myself. But his eyes are focused on Nathan. The man draws back his fist and sends it slamming into Nathan's jaw. I watch in horror as Nathan's eyes roll back in his head, the base of his skull hitting the wall. My arm is yanked back as Nathan hits the ground.

I duck down, making myself small. There's no way I can take this man in a physical fight. The best thing I can do is try to protect myself. But he doesn't hit me. He turns away, placing the gun back in its holster at his hip. Next to me, Nathan is out cold.

"Wait. Please tell me what's going on. Please. You don't have to do this." I reach out, grasping his ankle. "Don't leave us here like this. I know you're being used by her—"

He kicks his leg out, and I have to duck to keep his boot from colliding with my face. He wrenches free from my grasp and jabs the tip of his boot toward my face again, but he fortunately misses.

The man turns around, climbs the steps, and leaves. The storm door slams behind him with a final thud that rattles my bones. The lock clicks back in place.

I'm left with an unconscious Nathan and a bag of sandwiches on the dirty floor. I'm starving, but at the same time, I don't want to eat the food. I don't know where it came from, what it could be laced with.

I stare at the sandwiches, debating, my grumbling stomach wanting to answer for me. I decide I can't risk it.

"Nathan?" I press two fingers underneath his jaw and find a pulse. Then I turn him slightly so that he's in the recovery position.

Once he's okay, I maneuver myself lower to the ground, placing my cuffed wrist on the cement. The one thing I can do in this horrible place is work on getting my wrist out of this handcuff. I try it for a few seconds and then realize the masked man brought me something that could help. *The water.*

It takes a moment or two to reach the bag. I grab a bottle and pour some over my wrist, hoping it might provide lubrication. But it does little to speed up the process. The cuffs are on tight. My skin is red raw after being scraped by the metal.

Shit. Shit. Shit. Shit. Concentrate, Lucy. I pull. I tug. I cry. The pain is relentless, but I can't stop. I just want to be free from Nathan. I want a shot at protecting myself.

After about five minutes of agony, I wrestle them up to my knuckles, rubbing my hand raw. A trickle of blood runs down my wrist. *More lubrication*, I think morbidly. But I don't stop. I want the handcuffs off me before Nathan wakes up. Who knows if I might have to protect myself from *him* at some point in all this mess? He's not a man I can trust.

When my thumb pops out of its socket, I swallow down a scream. My vision blurs, and I'm forced to bite my lip to remain conscious. Sweat beads across my forehead, and I suck in sharp breaths, tasting blood. The cuff slips off nice and easy once my thumb is dislocated, though my pinky is red and bruised in the process. I'm careful to place the cuff down on the ground gently, and then I straighten up. I get to my feet and stretch my legs, feeling them wobble beneath my body, unsure of my weight.

I don't want to try to pop my thumb knuckle back into place, but if I wait, I'll lose my nerve. It takes three laps of the tiny room, pacing and mumbling to myself, to build up the nerve. Then I pull in a few deep breaths, take my fingers from my other hand, and pinch them against my thumb socket, trying to jam the digit back in place.

My breath hitches. I feel like someone rammed a hot needle into the thumb joint. Then I let go. Did it work? I'm not sure. The pain is still too bad for me to move the thumb, but it does look better and less like it's hanging off my hand. I slip down to the floor and rest my head against the wall. I'm free. It's such a small triumph, but here it is. I did one thing to help myself.

While Nathan is still unconscious, I walk over to the broken pieces of the camera and search for something sharp. But the sharp pieces are all too tiny, and the rest is blunt. I spend a few moments trying to snap a large piece in half but it's no good. Instead, scramble up to the door.

Four or five concrete steps lead up to the reinforced door, with a handrail on either side. On the top step, which is wide enough for two people to stand, I make myself as small as possible, wrapping my arm through the metal leg propping up the handrail. Crouched like a bug, I wait. The masked man never replaced the camera. I'm sure that was the point of the food—to knock us out so he could replace it while we sleep. That means he'll be back, and he'll expect us to be stupid enough to eat that food. Soon, the door is going to open. Someone will return. And when they do, I'll be waiting in the shadows to ambush them.

31

My chin drops as I surrender to sleep. Then I blink myself awake, jerking my head. My hand throbs, and I concentrate on it, forcing myself to stay conscious. I need to be alert.

Nathan remains unconscious, but I've at least seen him move once or twice. I know he's alive, but I'm concerned. After all, he did hit his skull on the way down. Concussion is no joke. Some people never recover, and others live with life-altering brain damage.

A thought runs through my mind: *If that's what he did to Nathan, what will he do to me?* Maybe he'll want to have fun with me before he kills me. It all depends on what Angela has asked for. God, I want to see her. I want to know why. What made her like this? Did someone corrupt her—ski-mask man—or did she corrupt him? Maybe I'll never know.

I pull my thoughts back to the room. Obviously, if this man can knock Nathan out with a single punch, my best bet is to be sneaky. Brute force will never get me out of here.

There's a scratching. It's quiet. Metal on metal. I shift

myself, hanging half off the step, clinging to the handrail as someone on the other side of that door unlocks it with a key. My pulse pounds as the door slowly rises to reveal the silhouette of the ski-mask man.

If he notices me, he doesn't react. He pauses as if listening for our movements. I glance at the room beyond where I'm huddled. With one slip, I would fall four feet onto the concrete. He'd hear that. I could breathe wrong, and he'd hear it. He's so close to me, I could reach out and touch him. If he turns his head to the left, and the moonlight falls through the door in exactly the right spot... I don't continue that thought. It's best not to consider every way this could go wrong.

He closes the door behind him, and my heart sinks. I hoped I could slip past him without him noticing, but he's too quick. Then he takes two more steps and pauses. He cocks his head, staring as if he's trying to figure out why Nathan is alone. The man clutches a screwdriver in one hand and a new camera in the other. Nathan was right about the camera.

I swallow hard as the man slowly turns around. He's still wearing the mask, so I don't have a decent shot at identifying him if I'm ever able to break free and get help. Now is my only chance. He's there, alone, gun still holstered, his hands full of equipment.

I take a giant leap from the top step, springing onto the guy's back. I bend my arm around his neck to choke him. The sudden movement causes my bad hand to throb, but I ignore it, gritting my teeth and applying as much pressure as I can.

The ski-mask man staggers backward, and I almost lose my grip. I hook my legs around his torso, trying to hook my ankles together. It helps keep him from accessing his gun as his arms flail. When he jams the screwdriver against my thigh, it doesn't puncture the skin, but it hurts like hell, and I cry out in pain. I throw my weight from side to side, trying to get him off balance. As his arms come out to steady himself, I hear the screwdriver clank against the concrete.

I'm torn. I'm not strong enough to choke this man out, but if I drop to the floor to get the screwdriver, I give him an opportunity to get his gun. I'm not sure I can reach down to his holster and keep hold of him. But I have to try.

He yanks his elbow up and back, clipping my left ear. Immediately, I reach down with my free arm, my hand still throbbing from the thumb dislocation, and grunt as I make a grab for his gun. He knows what I'm doing and throws his head back, connecting his skull with my top lip. I feel it burst, and warm blood trickles down my chin. My fingers brush the gun, but I don't reach it. Before he can throw me off, I try one more time and grasp it for a dizzying second before I'm launched backward. The gun flies from my hand as I land with a *thump* against the concrete. I hear it skittering across the floor somewhere in the shelter.

Our eyes lock in the dark. Both of us are winded. Both of us are determined to survive this. I scuttle up and reach for the gun. He grabs my ankle, but I kick him squarely in the nose with my free leg.

But he still has hold of me. His weight travels up my body until he's lying on top of me, and I can smell the bitter coffee on his breath.

"She didn't say you'd be this lively," he says.

He grabs my hair at the nape of my neck and pulls my head up. I know my face is about to smash into the concrete, and I can't... I whimper. He does it once, and pain erupts through my nose and forehead.

Then he spins me around so we're face-to-face. "You're

making this harder than it needs to be. You should've eaten your sandwich. I made it special for you."

"Angela won't give you what you want," I say, grasping at any old straw. "Me and Nathan. We're the rich ones. We'll pay you double."

He laughs. His hands wrap around my throat. I gurgle as he applies pressure. My hands fly up to my neck, and my fingernails dig into his flesh. It does nothing. But as he chokes me, I notice a glint of metal against the concrete floor. The screwdriver. I let go of his hands and reach out. My fingers fumble. I stretch my arm out as far as it'll go.

The ski-mask man's stormy blue-gray eyes are bloodshot, but a twinkle of excitement glints across them. He enjoys this, and he waits for the life to leave my body. This man is a psychopath, excited to be the one to take my life from me. My lungs burn as his grip tightens. And as the world starts to go dark, the hand groping out across the concrete floor finally chances upon the ridged plastic of a screwdriver handle. Quietly, I slip it into my fist. Black dots play across my vision. I'm on the verge of unconsciousness. I may only have one attempt to defend myself before the world around me goes black.

I shove the screwdriver up toward his neck, but my aim is off. It doesn't hit his jugular or even a main artery. It doesn't even break the skin. He flinches but doesn't let go. I take another stab at his neck. I leave welts, and the tender flesh around the side of his neck is already showing signs of blueish-black bruising.

He puts up a good fight, but so am I. He grunts in pain and thrashes against me, bucking his head side to side to avoid the screwdriver blows. He grits his teeth. I keep stabbing. He grips my neck harder, refusing to give up until he's finished the job.

My vision blinks in and out. This is it. My arm flops to the floor. The last bit of energy zaps out of me. I don't have the strength to keep fighting.

32

It's a relief to let go. All the fear and pain subside. A woman smiles at me from the other side of my prison. Mom. I want to reach out and touch her face, but I can't. I'm still pinned to the floor by this man.

Finally, his hands release me. I find it strange that I feel him let me go. Then something flutters against the delicate skin beneath my eyes, and it occurs to me that I'm not dead after all. I don't know where the strength to open my eyes comes from, but the first thing I see is the ski mask slipping from my attacker. I'm offered the first glimpse of his face.

The man has straw-textured chin-length hair. Messy tendrils frame his thin face. His skin is clear but dirty, perhaps from being under the mask for so long. For some reason, his neck arches back, like he's being pulled from behind.

Some of the weight lifts from my body, and I shuffle out from under him. Then I understand what's happening. Nathan is on top of the man, arms wrapped around his neck. I don't waste any time. I run over to the part of the shelter I saw the gun fly to and search for it.

My windpipe feels dented. My throat is sore and bruised. But I'm still alive. I get on all fours and grope the concrete. Behind me, I hear the grunts of the two men as they fight. I don't think Nathan has the upper hand anymore. We need a weapon.

I'm all the way in the back corner when my hand finds the cool metal of the gun. My finger brushes the trigger as I grab it, and I slow down my movements, forcing myself to be deliberate, to *think*, to not let the urgency of the situation force me into rash decisions. Our lives depend on what I do next.

When I turn around, I do so with the gun between both hands. My gunmanship involved a thirty-minute crash course with my dad when I was eighteen years old. But what I do remember is where the safety is and where the trigger is. Gently, I click off the safety.

Nathan is like a rag doll, half-collapsed against the floor, with the ski-masked man punching him in the face. Aiming at the man is too risky. I could kill Nathan in the process. But I see that our attacker is distracted. He's in his violent element, pounding and pounding his victim.

Quietly, I walk over to him, and I aim the gun at the base of his skull. "Stop," I croak. "Or I'll blow your fucking head off."

He stops. Nathan flops to the concrete, a dribble of bloody saliva pooling on the ground.

"I don't think you will, Lucy. I don't think you're a killer." The man straightens up to full height, forcing me to raise the gun to track with his movements.

"I'll do anything to get out of here," I say, my throat raw and burning. "You've got us locked up like animals. What happens when you corner an animal?"

Something about his demeanor makes me think he's smiling, even though I can't see his face. *Who is this man? Why is he here, doing Angela's dirty work?*

He backs *into* my gun, and my heart pounds. He forces me backward. My finger approaches the trigger, but he ducks down then spins, kicking me straight in the abdomen. I'm on the floor again, and he looms over me, his hand outstretched for the gun. I can't stand the thought that he might win. I can't die in this dirty storm shelter. And with that thought, I pull the trigger.

The sound is deafening in the tiny room. For at least three seconds, I can't hear a single thing due to the screeching ring in my ears. But I do see him take the bullet in his shoulder. I see him stagger back in surprise. But what he really doesn't expect is the second bullet aimed right for his chest. He hits the ground and lies there in a bloody puddle.

I don't want to watch him die, which he's surely going to do because I don't think anyone could lose that much blood and survive. My mind asks, *What have you done? Lucy, what have you done? Did you need to kill him?*

Fuck. I shouldn't feel guilty. I push the thoughts away and reach for Nathan's hand, helping him up from the floor. He's unsteady but manages to walk a few steps.

He glances down at his wrist. The handcuff is still linked around it. His eyes trail to me. "How did you get free?"

"I dislocated my thumb."

He stares at me in disbelief, then we stagger toward the shelter door. As we pass the man, I see him cough up blood then shudder from his head to his feet. A second later, he grows limp. His eyes are still open wide, alarmed.

"I did that," I say, more to myself than Nathan.

"You had to. There was no other choice. Don't worry—I'll testify for you if you're worried about the police."

I never want to hear Nathan tell me not to worry again. I do not trust an iota of what this man says. But I just nod.

"We've got to get out of here," Nathan says. "He must have a set of keys in his pocket. I'll check for ID, too."

"Make sure he's dead. We don't want him chasing us out of here." I've seen enough horror movies to make sure that doesn't happen.

Nathan nods and wipes some of the blood from his face before he kneels down next to the man. He feels for a pulse, checks his pockets, then holds up a bunch of keys on a shamrock keyring. I help Nathan back on his feet.

"You all right?" I ask. "Do we need to find bandages for those cuts?" I desperately need water. I also think I could sleep for a month, but getting out is our priority.

"One thing at a time. Let's get out of here."

He leans some of his weight on my shoulders as we inch our way up the steps to the shelter door. I want to check over my shoulder, terrified of the ski-masked man coming back to life. But the only sounds in the small space are my rasping breath and Nathan's unsteady footsteps. He passes me the keys, and I unlock the door, pulling in a lungful of air as it opens.

As soon as we step out on solid ground, Nathan strips his bloody shirt off. He wipes the blood from his face and tosses the shirt in the grass. Dawn is about to break. The sky hangs heavy and low, gloomy with a hint of orange creeping in at the edges.

There's a small brick house a few yards from the storm shelter. It has a wooden porch on the brink of collapse. A hole-riddled screen door bangs against its frame.

Nathan blinks at me. "Do you think that guy lived here?"

"I guess so. Jesus, where are we?" I walk a few paces toward the building. All around us is scrubby grass with no other properties and a few long-stretching roads. "We're in the middle of nowhere."

I lift my head to the sky, the breeze tickling the baby hairs at the nape of my neck. My throat aches. This isn't the triumphant escape I hoped it would be.

"We need to get inside that house," Nathan says. "We need water. And painkillers."

I stare at the house. Something about it makes my spine shiver. From the closed drapes to the broken window on the first floor, it doesn't feel right. But what choice do we have?

33

"Vivian could be in there," Nathan says, cutting through my thoughts.

"You mean your blackmailing buddy?" I roll my eyes. "Yay."

"I'm worried about her." He takes a step toward the house. "You don't know what could have happened to her. Angela could have her locked up."

"Wait. Angela could be in there. Or that guy's family."

Nathan stumbles back to me. "Give me the gun."

I glance down at my right hand. I completely forgot I was holding it, and that disturbs me so much, I could throw it on the ground. Instead, I pass it to Nathan and nod for him to continue toward the house. While he gets closer, I tuck myself behind an old truck parked down the drive.

Nathan cups his hands over his eyes and pushes his face toward the window, attempting to peer through a single crack in the drapes.

"Can you see anything in there?" I call out behind him.

Nathan straightens his spine and turns around, shaking his head. "It's too dark in there, but I don't see movement. No lights are on."

I swallow hard and shift my weight. I'm getting restless, desperate to get out of here. Nathan puts his hand over the doorknob and gives it a little twist. "The door is locked, too."

He walks to the side of the porch and plants his hands on the railing. He cranes his neck to the side yard, checking beyond the front of the building. Then he returns to the porch and slams his body against the door. It crunches under his weight, swinging open.

"Problem solved," he says with a smile.

Nathan disappears into the house. I wonder what he'll do if he finds his wife in there. *Is he cold enough to kill her? And do I really believe his story about him and Vivian being in love? What if all of this was him and Angela?*

No, it can't be. The fight in the shelter was real. Nathan really thought he was going to die.

I check the area again. The sun rises, brightening the dim light, and I can see that nothingness stretches for mile. An unidentifiable green crop grows in identical rows. Then I spot a two-lane road a few yards behind the property. It's eerily similar to the place Nathan and I were caught having sex—which led to me shooting a man in the chest about a month later.

My throat is tight, and my eyes flood with tears. It hits me —I took a life. But I killed him to save us both. I did what I had to do.

I turn to the house, squinting, wishing the drapes were open so I could see Nathan moving through the place. If he doesn't return, I need a backup plan. My attention turns to the truck. It's an old rust bucket. There's no way I'd be able to drive it without the keys. I can't hotwire a vehicle, and if I tried, it would be a waste of time. My best bet would be to run down that road and either hide in the tall crops in the adjacent fields or try to flag down a car.

The front door of the house opens, and he pokes his head out. "There's no one here. Come on, it's safe. We'll get some supplies and get out of here."

"Nathan, are we in the same area that we… you know? We had sex in your car?"

He gazes out at the fields beyond. "It's hard to tell. I don't know. Maybe."

"Who knew we'd be having sex there at that moment? Vivian?"

He swallows, his face stonelike. "Yes."

"She was waiting with a camera to catch us in the act. And how did Angela find out about us? Because she sure seemed to have a lot of time to plan all of this out. Is it possible that Vivian went to Angela?"

Nathan sighs. "Why would she do that?"

"I don't know. So she could keep all the cash for herself? To watch us die? I don't know. But it seems weird that we're in the same place as last time."

"Yeah. I guess things got out of control."

"Out of control? The mother of your children locked us in a bunker, and we had to kill our way out."

"You're not helping, Lucy. Do you know how much I'm trying not to think about my kids right now? If I do, I'll lose it. I don't know what she's done to them!"

"I'm sorry," I say. "I didn't realize that. For what it's worth, I don't think Angela would harm them. Plus, they weren't at your house the day she drugged me."

"Maybe she took them to her sister's," he says. "I hope so."

I step into the house and immediately flinch at the stench of decay. Whoever had us trapped in his storm shelter lived like an absolute pig. Moldy bread sits out on the counter.

"I think this person was motivated by money," Nathan says. "Look how he lived. I can't see them being in a relationship. I bet Angela hired him."

We pick our way through ski-mask man's belongings, searching for a phone, fresh bottled water, car keys, fresh food, anything. In the end, I fill up a canteen from the faucet and find a bag of Cheetos to eat. Nathan grabs a T-shirt from a pile of clean laundry, eats some dry cereal, and shares some water with me. We find a password-protected laptop and a passcode-protected mobile phone. When Nathan tries to call 911, the service cuts out.

"Let's get in the truck and get out of here," I suggest. "Are the keys on the bunch you found in his pocket?"

"I guess we'll find out," Nathan says. On the way out he grabs the laptop. "If he is in contact with my wife, I guess the evidence will be on here."

I open a drawer in the messy living room and lift out an ID card. "Samuel Wayne. I guess we know his name now."

Those Cheetos sit sourly in the pit of my stomach. I know the name of the man I killed. *In self-defense*, I remind myself.

Nathan reaches the truck before I do and tries the keys. The door opens, and he slaps it with delight. "Let's get this baby running!"

Climbing into the truck, I brush dust away from my skirt. I haven't felt this filthy since I got pushed into a mud puddle in third grade. Nathan inserts the key and turns it. It starts, chokes, and gives up with a splutter.

"Hit the gas," I say.

He tries it again, revving the engine. It's promising for a moment, turning over, hitting a bit of a rhythm, and then it dies again.

"Fuck!" Nathan slams the wheel. "The battery's dead. We're going to have to walk."

34

Dawn breaks as we walk. Nathan has the laptop tucked under his arm, and I keep the phone in one hand and the canteen of water in the other. The road is up ahead, stretching for miles. We walk in silence for a long time, the only sound our footsteps moving against the gritty asphalt. Nathan stares straight ahead. I can't stop checking over my shoulder to make sure we're not being followed. I can't shake the idea that Vivian had something to do with this. There are too many interconnected parts. I keep picturing her hiding somewhere in that house, waiting for the right moment to strike.

After walking about three miles, we come to a four-way intersection. I'm parched and take a sip of water before passing it to Nathan.

"It's going to bake out here later," he says. "We've got a few hours before it gets warm, I reckon. Any signal on the phone?"

I try the emergency-service function on the phone again, but this time, the battery dies.

"Shit," Nathan says. "Piece-of-shit phone."

"We can go back. Charge it up and then come back out here."

"Is that what you want to do?"

I glance back in the direction of the house. "No. I want to get away from here."

We collect ourselves and keep trudging on. After about another mile, we come to another intersection. At the stop sign, Nathan reads the street names. His eyes flash with excitement, and he points at them.

"This is Route 64!"

"It is? So we are close to where we broke down that day."

"Yeah," Nathan says. "We're closer to civilization than I thought."

Route 64 leads into Chicago. But I don't recognize anything around me, so we must be miles out of the city. And now we need to know which direction to take.

We hesitate, debating, but the sound of an engine quiets us. Nathan grabs my arm in an almost involuntary way. Then he leaps out into the road. I follow him, hearing the engine coming closer. I see the vehicle in the distance.

"Hey!" Nathan yells.

The driver has no choice but to stop, and the dark-blue sedan slowly comes to a halt. The driver opens his window and gives us a guarded look. "What the hell happened to you two?"

Nathan and I exchange a glance. We only have about ten seconds to make something up on the fly before this guy gets too suspicious and drives away. Who would want to pick up two beaten up people talking about being locked in a storm shelter by a psychopath?

"We got mugged," Nathan says, throwing his arms up in

the air. "Wouldn't you know it. First our car broke down so we were left in the middle of nowhere. And then these thugs just jumped us."

The man narrows his eyes, glancing between us. Both his hands are on the wheel. "Where's your car at, then?"

I lick my lips and point in the opposite direction, careful not to give this stranger any clues. He has a long, wiry gray beard, but he's bald. He's thin, but he has black-inked tattoo sleeves on both arms that are stretched from the loosen skin of old age. His face is tan and weathered like he's spent a lot of time out in the sun over the years.

"We've walked five miles," Nathan says. "We're exhausted and my... my wife needs medical attention. Come on, man, we just need a ride into town."

The man studies us, debating. "I'm heading that way now. Sure. Why the hell not? You guys seem like you've had a rough time. It'll be my good deed for the day."

Nathan and I breathe a collective sigh of relief and jump into the backseat. The man peers at us through the rearview mirror, but it's more out of curiosity than suspicion.

Nathan leans forward. "This is going to sound even crazier than we probably already look, but we left our cell phones back at the car by accident. Do you mind if I borrow yours for a minute?"

"You left your phones?" The man's eyebrows arch quizzically as if he believed everything we told him up to the point where we *both* left our phones behind.

Nathan and I shrug, releasing simultaneous nervous chuckles. "Just the stress, I guess."

The man studies us a moment more, but his face relaxes. The lies get easier to say, but they never get easier to carry around. I've learned this the hard way ever since I slept with Nathan.

Nathan enters 911, and then his thumb deletes it, and he punches in a different number instead.

"What are you doing?" I mouth.

"Calling Vivian," he whispers.

The windows are down in the front of the car, and the breeze blows my hair around. I tuck it in my hand to keep it in place and watch Nathan.

After a few seconds, he closes his eyes and shakes his head. "No answer."

I meet the driver's eyes through the mirror. "Can you drop us off here?" We've been in the car for about twenty minutes now. We never would have made it without this ride.

"Here?" The man points to the road.

We're on the outskirt of a town I recognize, and I'm pretty sure there's a mechanic's shop just up ahead. We can get out of this car and phone the police from there. It's a perfect setup.

Nathan's eyes brighten as he catches on to my idea. "Thank you so much. I'd offer to pay you, but I don't have any cash."

"Don't worry about it." The man waves a dismissive hand and pulls up to the curb.

Nathan's hand is already on the door handle, opening the door, before the man even comes to a full stop.

"Thank you again." I slide across the seat and exit the vehicle. "Come on," I tell Nathan. My legs are tired, but I'm motivated by the fact that we're so close to the police station now. "We're going inside, and we're telling them everything."

Nathan's forehead wrinkles, and he scrunches up his face as he shakes his head.

I give him an appalled chuckle, tossing my hands up in the air. I've resigned myself to the fact that Nathan is going to argue with everything I say. "You can do whatever you want, Nathan, but I've already made my choice."

"It's not that." He frowns.

I pause, but I'm wired with adrenaline and frustrated by his hesitation.

His eyes are pitiful as he gazes up at me and blinks. "What about Vivian?"

"What about her?" I shrug.

"She didn't answer the phone when I called her."

"She doesn't recognize the number—it's not that big of a deal."

Nathan shakes his head, his expression grim. "No. I'm worried. If she knew I was missing, she'd answer any strange number just in case."

I regard him. He isn't the man I thought he was. It's been clear for a while, but it still hits me with a sense of poignancy —Nathan was never interested in me. Everything he's done during and since the retreat has been for Vivian. Even now, he's more obsessed with finding her than he is about speaking to his children.

I shake my head sadly, glad that I'm not him. "You can stand on the sidewalk and be worried all you want, then. I'm going to the police for help."

35

Leaving Nathan on the sidewalk might have been selfish, but I didn't care. Getting away from him allowed me to breathe again. I'll never forget the looks on the mechanics' faces as I stumbled into their shop and told them to call the police. Two minutes later, I was sitting in their reception area with a woman called Claire and a cup of mint tea.

Now I'm staring at the wall in the emergency room, waiting again. I would nap, but every time I close my eyes, I see him—Samuel Wayne, the ski-mask man.

The partition slides open, and my body reacts. Detective Higgins lifts his hands to apologize and walks in. His broad shoulders squeeze into the examination room through a narrow slit in the curtain.

He gestures to the splint on my hand. "How you holding up?"

"Well," I say, "I dislocated a thumb getting out of a pair of handcuffs. And I had my face smashed into concrete by a psycho but still got away. So watch out. I'm a lively one." I feel the blood drain from my face as I remember Samuel saying the same thing to me as his coffee breath tickled my ears.

"I'm sorry to hear that, Ms. Croft. I know you've been through a lot in the last forty-eight hours."

"Tell me about it," I mumble.

"I wanted to come and check on you and give you an update on the case." Detective Higgins gestures to a chair next to the wall. "May I?"

I nod. "Sure."

He sits down with an exaggerated sigh.

"Where's Nathan?" I ask.

"He's in another examination room, getting checked out for injuries."

"Oh." My eyes fall to my lap.

"Is it painful?" Higgins points at my splint.

"Yup."

Detective Higgins releases a boisterous chuckle that helps me lower my guard a bit. "I'll bet. I've never seen anyone successfully get out of a handcuff like that before."

This makes me smile and gives my ego a little boost. "Well, I'm not just anyone."

"Clearly."

"I've made a few mistakes," I admit, my eyes welling.

Detective Higgins gives me a sympathetic frown and reaches for a tissue. He plucks one from the box and hands it over to me. "We've all been there."

"Thanks," I mutter and dab my eyes and nose with the tissue, using my uninjured hand, then laugh at the irony. "But I don't think we've all been there."

Detective Higgins shrugs. "I've met a lot of people who have made a lot of mistakes."

"Sleep-with-our-married-boss types of mistakes? Shoot-a-man-in-the-chest kind of mistakes?"

Detective Higgins's face shifts to serious. "Right. About that second one. I don't think it's going to be a problem." He gestures to the ruby-red marks across my neck. "What with your injuries and Nathan's injuries and the fact that you were both locked up and cuffed, well, I think it's a pretty clear case of self-defense." He clears his throat. "Now, I have some unfortunate news to share."

"Lay it on me. I'm already neck-deep in bad news as it is."

"Well, it won't come as any surprise to you that Nathan's wife, Angela, is missing. We think she ran when she didn't hear from her hired thug. But Vivian Holbrook is also missing."

"Oh. Well, I guess that tracks. I mean, I wasn't sure, but I suspected she had something to do with us being incarcerated in that place. She and Nathan were having an affair. But I think someone told Angela about *me* and Nathan—before she found out during the investigation—and I think it might be Vivian."

"What makes you say that?" he asks.

"I don't know exactly. It might be an instinct. But I feel like Nathan isn't smart enough to embezzle money or black-mail me, and I think he was genuinely scared when he thought his son was missing at the park. I think Vivian might be the mastermind behind everything. And I wonder if she went to Angela to... I don't know, squeeze more cash out of them maybe?" I sigh. "There's a piece of the puzzle missing."

"If there is, we'll find it." Detective Higgins crosses one foot over his knee and clutches his ankle.

"Does Nathan know?" I ask.

"Yes."

"He's too deluded to think she'd betray him," I say, thinking aloud. "He probably thinks she's dead."

Detective Higgins leans forward. "We could do with someone like you on the job. You're pretty good at this."

I shake my head. "I wasn't before. I had to learn to be. I've never been so scared in my life these last few weeks."

"Lucy, it's over now."

But I don't think it is. Angela and Vivian are out there somewhere. Angela has tried to kill me once already. Who says she won't try again?

36

Higgins lets me know that Nathan is being cooperative with the police but that he's already lawyered up. He can't tell me much more about that. But it's pretty clear Nathan will be charged with blackmail and embezzlement. I'm glad to find out that he's seen his kids, though. Nathan is many things, but it would be cruel to keep him from them for any longer. I hope Angela's sister is a lot nicer than Angela.

"Please tell me you have some idea where Angela is?" I ask.

"At this moment, we don't know her whereabouts," he says. "I'm sorry—that's all I can tell you."

"Will Nathan have custody of his kids, with the embezzlement and everything?"

"I can't say what will happen with that yet. It'll be down to social services to make the call."

I regard Higgins. "What about the money—my dad's money?"

"It's gone," he says, his expression grim. "But we are investigating a digital trail that might lead us to it."

I drop my head into my hands. "Shit."

"We suspect Angela took it and fled, but of course, we have no proof of this yet. The forensics team is going through Vivian's house, as well as Nathan and Angela's home, searching for DNA evidence to link her to the crime."

"What about Samuel Wayne?"

"His body is being taken for autopsy. The property and the storm shelter all belonged to him. And between you and me, this guy was a bad dude. He has multiple assaults on his record. And we found his profile on the dark web. We found all sorts of weapons and cameras inside the house, so you guys had a lucky escape. Right now, we're processing everything. We might even find more."

"He was a hit man?" I ask, reading between the lines. I shudder, thinking about the fact that I was locked in a hit man's storm cellar and survived.

I rest my head on the back of the examination table and gaze up at the ceiling. The on-call physician enters the room to give me my discharge papers and instructions on how to take care of my hand splint.

Detective Higgins stands and fastens the bottom button of his blazer. He nods his chin to me. "I'll be in touch if I have any questions or if we receive any new information that might be helpful in this case."

"Thank you." I offer him a kind smile, hoping it's not too stiff.

Mrs. Doebler waves to me as I unlock the condo and head inside. She doesn't ask what happened to me and why I have a splint on my hand. Maybe she doesn't notice.

At the hospital, I decided not to call my dad. I only needed treatment for my thumb and throat. I didn't want him hurrying down here to be at my bedside. Plus, I needed a minute to myself.

I'm no longer afraid to tell him what happened. The events of the last forty-eight hours have made me realize what matters. I think of Nathan in the storm cellar, never giving up on his love for Vivian but barely thinking of his children. I think of Angela doing all of this for revenge—the sickness and darkness that must be inside her.

I want no part of that. Whatever is in the water here, I'm done with it. There's not much point drafting a resignation letter to the firm. Maybe Chet will call me tomorrow and ask me if I'm okay. Maybe he won't. Maybe I'll be gone tomorrow. I don't want to stay here, wondering when Angela might pop out from the shadows.

I keep trying to put myself in Angela's shoes, to figure out why she could possibly be the way she is. All I can think is that she is obsessed—with revenge, with Nathan's infidelity, perhaps even with me. The thought makes me shiver. She's still out there.

The one good thing to have come out of all this is that I've shaken my own destructive obsession. I'm not the same person I was at the retreat. And I'll never let that kind of obsession consume me ever again.

Before my imagination runs wild, I grab the landline I rarely use and dial my dad's number.

"Lucy," he says. "My God, I've been trying to call you."

"I'm so sorry, Dad."

"Are you okay?"

"I'm fine, but a lot has happened since we last spoke." I

pull in a deep breath. "I need to tell you some stuff, and it's not going to be easy to hear."

"I'm just relieved to hear your voice."

"Me too. And... would it be okay if I moved back home for a while?"

He sighs, and it isn't a frustrated sigh—it's one of pure relief. "Of course, it would, sweetheart."

"Thank you," I say, and then I launch into my story.

When I made my first mistake, I was grieving for my lost mom. I didn't know how to deal with the pain in my heart, and I made every wrong decision you could make. Little did I know, all I wanted to do was go home. And now I will.

EPILOGUE

It takes a bit of getting used to. Every time I pass a mirror, I get a jolt. My straight jet-black hair has been replaced with long, flowing, wavy blond locks. My new brown contact lenses and fake spray tan make me unrecognizable to even myself. But I like it. I'm stunning. And this new look is necessary. No one will find me here. No one will recognize me. No one will search for a tan, blond woman. They'll hunt for a woman who doesn't exist anymore, who faded away. I'm like a phoenix rising from the ashes. I am born anew.

I'm no longer Angela Robertson. I'm Megan Ashburn. And Megan Ashburn lives her life according to her own rules, her own ambitions. With no baggage, nothing holding her back. No responsibilities. Just a bright future ahead, a clean slate.

Satisfied with my reflection, I blow myself a kiss in the mirror and strut to my fifth-floor balcony that overlooks the pool in the coastal community where I now live. From here, I have a clear view of the beach beyond the horizon line of sand dunes and palm trees.

I stop in my kitchen and pour myself a glass of chardonnay before sliding the balcony door open. I sit in one of my outdoor lounge chairs and gaze down at the pool. It's more crowded than usual for this time of night.

A child is squealing and crying, stomping his foot, and having a meltdown over something while his frazzled mother holds out a snack. He throws it on the ground and jumps in the water. Her hair is messy, and there are dark circles beneath her eyes. I don't envy her. I don't miss the meltdowns either. I was never much of a parental figure. I had to learn as I went, but I never connected to my twins in the way a mother is supposed to. Neither of us had really wanted children, but when I got pregnant, we were forced into the roles, having to step up and endure the sleepless nights, the tantrums, the round-the-clock feedings and screaming. The incessant whining never ended. I much prefer the silence that I now enjoy.

I sigh and prop my legs up on the little bistro table in front of me. The beachy breeze tickles my cheeks. I inhale a deep breath of sea air, embracing the saltiness of it through my pores. This has been the best few weeks of my life. I had years to prepare for this moment, and now that it's here, I relish it. The peace and serenity have enveloped me, and I embrace every second of the bliss.

Nathan began sleeping with Vivian when the twins were around a year old. Our marriage had started taking hits right after they were born, and it got worse and worse over time.

I'd always suspected Nathan was a weak man, and the affair confirmed it. But he never suspected a thing about me. He didn't know my strength equaled his weakness.

I watched Nathan and Vivian piss all my money away

month after month. The anger stayed dormant inside me. I had to keep it suppressed. If I didn't, the revenge wouldn't be as sweet. I couldn't afford to make careless mistakes. I had to be calculated, set my targets high, wait it out.

In the end, I got my victory and my quiet life with my fresh start. It was worth it.

Nathan's gambling addiction grew worse and worse. And Vivian didn't help. In fact, she enabled him, adding fuel to the fire. I couldn't stand by and do nothing.

He'll have to raise those brats all by himself. I'm done.

"You opened the chardonnay without me," she says, stepping out onto the balcony.

Red suits her. I smile and pass her the bottle. "Help yourself."

Right from the start, I figured Vivian was using him. There was far too much money disappearing each month for this to just be some overzealous gambling. She stole from us, and I intended to get it back.

I went to Vivian directly, and we talked. It was tense. Part of me wanted to kill her. But then she said three little words: "Let's kill him."

We became fast friends after that. She told me her plans to get even more money out of Nathan because she was pretty sure she could manipulate him into blackmail and embezzlement. She needed a mark—someone stupid enough to have sex with him.

Lucy.

No one would figure out that Vivian and I were friends. We met miles away from home. I made up excuses that Nathan didn't care about—book clubs, brunch, anything that didn't involve much money because then he'd be asking questions. Anything about *me*, about who I was and what I did, never mattered to him.

Vivian told me about a man on the dark web who had a storm shelter. He didn't give us his name, but on the night I drugged Nathan, he turned up in a ski mask and carried him away. I gave him the camera to install. I wanted to watch my husband die. I was owed that. Then I duped that bitch, Lucy, by playing the part of a distraught wife wanting to put the broken pieces of her family back together.

Vivian took the money and ran before I left. All I had to do was wait for Lucy and Nathan to die of starvation and thirst in that storm cellar. Then I'd be finally free from the chains that bound me.

But those plans went awry. Nathan broke the camera, and I no longer had access to their death. As much as I wanted to see my revenge plan through, I knew it wasn't smart to wait around town any longer. I had my doubts about the man Vivian had hired. He was a scrawny thing, and I worried Nathan would overpower him. If they were smart enough to smash the camera, what else could they do? So I ran.

I'm Megan Ashburn, thanks to the ID we purchased. Vivian is Catherine Bolton. We haven't even left the US, simply traveled out of state.

Vivian chinks my wineglass with her own. We have a duffle bag with over a hundred thousand dollars in the safe in our rental. It's all the money she stole from Nathan over the years, along with Lucy's ransom money and everything Nathan embezzled from the company. We put down the first month's deposit in cash. Untraceable.

"To new beginnings," she says.

"To new beginnings," I say.

We watch the sun disappear behind the ocean's teal horizon. I've never really felt guilt about anything, and I certainly don't feel it now. Nathan and Lucy deserved what they got. When I close my eyes, I picture them handcuffed together in that little room. I hope they did rot in there. I'll thrive on that thought for as long as I'm alive. I hope I never find out either way.

AUTHOR BIO

SL Harker was raised on Point Horror books and loves thrills and chills. Now she writes fast-paced, entertaining psychological thrillers.

Stay in touch through her website: https://www.slharker.com/

Join the mailing list to keep up-to-date with new releases and price reductions.

ALSO BY SL HARKER

The New Friend

The Work Retreat

Printed in Great Britain
by Amazon